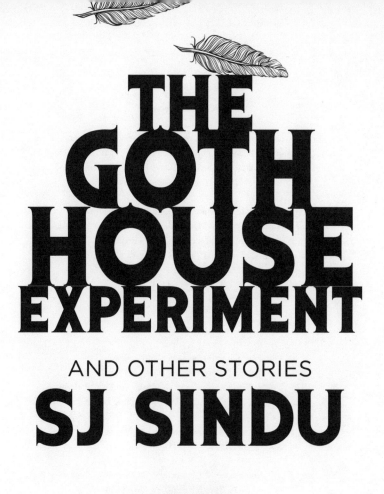

THE GOTH HOUSE EXPERIMENT

AND OTHER STORIES

SJ SINDU

SOHO

These stories first appeared, at times in different form, in the following: "Patriots'
Day" in *Fifth Wednesday Journal*; "I Like to Imagine Daisy from *Mrs. Dalloway* as
an Indian Woman" in *apt.*; "Wild Ale" in Electric Literature; "The Goth House
Experiment" in Queen Mob's Teahouse; "Miracle Boy" in *Fiction Vortex*.

Published by
Soho Press, Inc.
227 W 17th Street
New York, NY 10011

Library of Congress Cataloging-in-Publication Data
Names: Sindu, SJ, author.
Title: The goth house experiment : and other stories / SJ Sindu.
Description: New York, NY : Soho, [2023] | Identifiers: LCCN 2023018397

ISBN 978-1-64129-519-2
eISBN 978-1-64129-520-8

Subjects: LCGFT: Short stories. | Classification: LCC PS3619.I5688 G68 2023
| DDC 813/.6—dc23/eng/20230519
LC record available at https://lccn.loc.gov/2023018397

Interior design by Janine Agro
Feather illustration: © Vecteezy.com

Printed in the United States of America

10 9 8 7 6 5 4 3 2 1

For Sam

THE GOTH HOUSE EXPERIMENT

AND OTHER STORIES

TABLE OF CONTENTS

DARK ACADEMIA AND THE LESBIAN MASTERDOC

The day I found out about Dorothy was also the day my husband Dillon went on his first date as a man. Five years together, and one morning he'd woken up and decided it was time he tasted the single life from the male side. I'd arranged my face in an approximation of shock and indignation, before reversing and trying to look supportive.

"You can date, too," he said. He self-consciously pulled his T-shirt away from his chest, a habit he'd continued even after top surgery a year ago. "I know you miss dating women."

"Do I?" I imagined going out to the bars again, squeezing myself into the disco-ball miniskirts I'd worn in my twenties, dancing like I had when I was single, trying to gather up the energy to get to know someone new. That insufferable tango of disclosure and anxiety, the wondering and staring at the phone, the text messages drafted and deleted.

"You don't hate me for this, right?" Dillon rolled up the hem of his shirt and then rolled it back down. "You're really okay with me seeing other people?"

I splashed a smile over my face and took his hand from his shirt. "New adventures."

LATER, DILLON SUGGESTED I download Sapphyc, a dating app for women and femmes interested in each other.

"I don't do social media," I said. I lounged on our bed, scrolling through his Tinder profile while he tried on an endless series of outfits. I knew it was cliché to "not do social media." But I considered myself a gold star. I hadn't ever had a profile, not even on Myspace in high school or Facebook in college.

I swiped right and left on the potential paramours that popped up. Super glam brown woman who looked a little like me, her hair waving in the wind on a mountaintop. Reject. Cute stud with locks in a flannel shirt. Approve. Straight-looking guy holding a fish.

"Do you want to date a penis?" I asked. I shimmied my posture to relieve the cramps that had started a few days earlier.

"It's not social media. It's a dating app. It's different." Dillon modeled his first outfit: a tight long-sleeve shirt and ripped pants, converse high-tops with rainbow laces. "Does this say casual yet sexy? You know what, never mind." He pulled off the shirt and rummaged around in his closet. "How do you know he's a penis?"

I showed him the profile picture. Wraparound sunglasses. Patriots windbreaker. "He's holding a dead fish."

"Yikes."

"Is that a yikes no? Or a secret yikes yes?"

When Dillon didn't respond, I swiped "yes."

"Your scars are healing well," I said, watching the

long arch of Dillon's back as he bent over to grab something in our plastic drawers, the delicate bones of his spine pushing through the skin like islands in a long archipelago.

He paused, stood upright, and traced the lines on his chest, two identical straight scars where his breasts used to be. I'd once heard him at the beach telling a nosy older lady that the scars were the result of a double lung transplant.

"You think so? They're not too puffy?"

"Not at all." I swiped "no" on a few white femmes. "Try your old-man shirt."

Dillon grabbed a vintage silk dress shirt from a hanger and pulled it on. As he buttoned it up, he caught my eye in the mirror. "I know I keep asking, but you really haven't answered. Are you sure you're okay with me dating?"

I pretended to be engrossed in the app, folding my knees up to ease another cramp. "I'm not the jealous type," I said, cringing a little. Another cliché.

"That's still not really an answer."

THE COLD PAPER crinkled underneath my naked butt as I slid toward the edge of the examination table. The ultrasound technician waited for me, a white transducer wand in her hand.

"Right to the edge, love," she said, snapping her gum like a punctuation mark.

As I scooted, she slipped a condom onto the wand and swirled blue lubricant gel on the tip as if she were dispensing soft-serve ice cream into a cone.

"This might hurt a bit." She snapped her gum again and inserted the wand into my vagina.

I watched on the monitor, trying to ignore the pressure inside me, breathing through the cramps. For all his insistence on wanting to date as a man, Dillon didn't love using strap-ons. We had one—he'd gotten the harness custom fitted at the local sex shop by a girl with an asymmetrical haircut—but he rarely used it. My vagina wasn't used to anything larger than a few fingers, and that only rarely.

"Breathe," the technician said.

She moved the wand around, poking left and right.

I watched the grainy black-and-white pictures on the monitor. That was the inside of my uterus. Then, as she pushed toward my left ovary, a burst of color. She stopped, took a snapshot for the doctor, and made more colors flash. Snapshot. Colors. Snapshot.

"Is that bad?" I asked.

She wordlessly pointed at a handmade sign on the wall: TECHNICIANS ARE UNABLE TO DISCUSS THE FINDINGS OF YOUR ULTRASOUND. PLEASE WAIT FOR THE DOCTOR TO CONTACT YOU.

"But you've done a ton of these," I said. "Surely you know what the colors mean?" I tried to look trustworthy. "I'm just scared. Can you tell me?"

She pulled the wand out slowly, and I could breathe again.

"Please?"

"It might be a cyst," she said. She chewed, then snapped. "But the doctor will know. Looks like it's the size of a golf ball." She held out a wad of bleached white washcloths. "The doctor will call you on Tuesday for a diagnosis."

I sat up, dizzy. "Dorothy," I said. "I'll name it Dorothy." Dorothy the cyst who lived on my left ovary.

The technician shook the washcloths at me. "Why Dorothy?"

"My grandmother's name," I said. That wasn't true. Dorothy was the name my grandmother's Cambridge classmates had called her because they couldn't pronounce Draupadi.

What did the technician know, anyway? Dorothy could be benign. Or maybe Dorothy was cancer and I had only a few months to live.

AFTER MY ULTRASOUND, I sat under the awning of my local coffee shop while rain dripped cheerfully onto window-box geraniums. There was a problem with the sequence in the middle of my poetry manuscript. Something wasn't clicking. The resonance I'd hoped for the poems to have fell flat. I needed a complete reorder, but I was already a month past my deadline. My editor had emailed me that morning asking about the status of my book edits.

A gaggle of students approached, each dressed carefully in fast fashion designed to look like thrift-store clothing—plaid slacks that didn't fit, bottle glasses, gleaming white sneakers, oversize cable-knit sweaters frayed at the collar, tweed jackets with elbow patches.

Misty from my queer literature class was among them. She waved. Misty had announced during the first-day-of-class intros that she was an influencer who made videos about being sad. She was the clear center of the group, which appeared to be deliberately nearing my table.

I angled my laptop away.

"Writing poetry in a coffee shop on a rainy day," Misty said. "So dark academia of you, Dr. B."

Before I could ask what that meant, she turned away, tiny droplets of water shimmering on her shoulders. She led the rest of the students down the sidewalk and around the corner. They clustered in a group far closer than I'd ever walked with anyone, their heads tucked together and whispering.

DILLON CAME BACK from his date late, smelling of a cologne he didn't own. I was sitting in bed, preparing a lecture for my queer lit class.

"Shower," I said as soon as he burst through the bedroom door.

He seemed to glow with excitement under the warm light of our Ikea floor lamp. Before he'd brought up dating other people, I would fantasize about coming home and finding him with a stranger. The fear on his face, the fumbled apologies. His lover running out the door, clothes clutched in a fist. The righteous anger I'd be allowed to feel. Dillon following me around while I packed up my clothes, Dillon begging me to stay. Me, crying in a new, bare apartment, showering myself clean, and then slowly, slowly decorating with finds from the antique store down the street, getting a cat, settling into a new life. After I'd fully imagined the light fixtures I'd buy, I'd think of Dillon's lips, sucking the nipples of the stranger, and I'd masturbate.

Now, while I listened to the water cleanse him of

another human's cells and fluids, I tried to conjure up that image of Dillon with someone, to will myself wet. There was no stirring between my legs, no sign of interest, not even from Dorothy. The cramps were gone, as if now that I knew about Dorothy's existence, she didn't need to insist herself on my life anymore. She was just a ghostly, invisible presence, silently blooming poison into the rest of my body. I imagined the doctor's stony face telling me that I'd die before the end of the semester. I'd have to race to finish my manuscript. My only legacy. Even Dillon would soon forget me for his new lovers, finally able to live a fully unencumbered life without his pretransition past.

I closed my laptop, picked up my cell phone, and scrolled through the news. A coup in Southeast Asia. A Canadian election. People quitting academia in droves because of the state of the job market.

I clicked through a blog with a comment thread about how hard it was to get a professor job, how people who had been trying for seven or more years were just so tired they were giving up. Like staring at roadkill bursting open at the seams, I couldn't look away. I had my professor job. A good one, in fact. One that everyone in this comments section was hoping to get and couldn't. A nasty voice in my head told me that I'd worked hard because I was a queer brown femme and no one was going to give me anything just for existing, but I had this other voice in my head, too, a voice of gratitude telling me how lucky I was, that I should be grateful, not self-congratulatory. The nasty voice and the gratitude voice made an eerie chorus in my brain, egging each other on.

When Dillon was done showering, his black hair dripping and his skin smelling like Old Spice, we cuddled. He nestled into the crook of my armpit.

"How was it?" I asked.

"You don't want to know details, do you?"

"Just say it was fun."

"It was fun."

"Say thank you."

"Thank you."

I kissed the top of his head, inhaling the smell. A strange desperation climbed up inside me. "I love you," I said.

Dillon looked up, smiling like a baby. "Do you want to have some sexy time?"

I kissed him, hard. I tried to measure if he was kissing differently now that he'd probably kissed someone else, their DNA somehow changing his approach. He broke away and wiggled down, moving his face toward my crotch.

Sex—vigorous and loud, the kind where I'd be utterly obliterated—might be what it would take to wake Dorothy up so that I could feel her again.

"Hold me down," I said. "Fuck me."

Dillon's face flashed from surprise to annoyance.

"You know I don't like power play," he said.

I squashed the grunt of frustration that jumped into my throat. "Let's just cuddle," I said.

He moved back to my side and snuggled into me, humming happily.

MISTY WAS MY only office hours appointment on Monday. She came in with a sigh, looking like she'd walked off the set of an '80s movie about Oxford, and plopped down on the other side of my desk. She wound the ends of her sleek brown hair around and around her ringed finger.

"Dr. B," she sighed. "I've had a rough month."

I couldn't remember the particulars of her struggles, so I waited, nodding.

"I got scammed by that company that wanted me to be their brand ambassador?" she prompted, her eyes darting around my mostly empty office. "Did you just move in?"

"I like keeping my books at home," I said.

"You could really go wild if you wanted to." She pulled a coil of hair that she'd twisted with her fingers toward her shiny mouth and chewed on it. "Decorating, I mean. Yeah, you could have a real dark-academia vibe in here."

"We really should talk about when you'll be handing in your essay."

"There's tons of great ideas on TikTok." She gnawed on her hair like a goat. "Are you on TikTok?"

"I think I'm too old for TikTok."

Misty waved her hands in front of her face like she was blowing away a bad smell. "Bullshit, Dr. B. You should get on TikTok. It's a great way to promote your writing."

WHEN I GOT home, I googled "dark academia." Apparently, it was an "aesthetic," not in the philosophical way but as a synonym for an "aspirational lifestyle," complete with fashion videos, interior-design mood boards, and guidelines on proper activities. Other aesthetics included cottagecore, in which upper-middle-class kids wore linen, baked bread from scratch, and pretended to live without electricity in small, rough-hewn homes in the woods, Thoreau-style. But dark academia was all about mahogany bookshelves crammed with leather-bound tomes, their gilded spines glinting in dim light. Stone buildings with Gothic spires reaching into the sky. Brown tweed, slouchy turtlenecks, leather belts, book bags. One site suggested "dark academia hobbies" like writing to your past self and sealing the note with wax, smelling the pages of old books, pressing flowers into fountain-pen-inked journals, and writing poetry in coffee shops.

It was again like looking at roadkill—an unbidden, repulsive fascination. Young people playacted as professors of literature, history, and classics. TikTok's format of fifteen- and thirty-second videos encouraged the kind of unnuanced, uncritical engagement where dark academia flourished.

I click-holed for hours, until Dillon came home. He turned on the light in the kitchen where I sat with a beer.

"Why are you sitting in the dark?" He dumped the empty contents of his lunch bag into the sink, where I'd already put my dishes to soak. He folded up the sleeves of his button-down shirt and started rinsing plates.

"It's all Donna Tartt's fault," I said. "Dark academia. That's all I can gather."

"I have a second date," he said. "Donna Tartt the author?"

"Dark academia. They're all obsessed with it. My students. They like Donna Tartt's *The Secret History* and they grew up watching Harry Potter and now they're all obsessed with dusty books and English prep-school uniforms and the library from *Beauty and the Beast*."

Dillon loaded the plates all wrong, stacking them too close for them to get clean. "Sounds harmless. The date is Saturday. That okay?"

I joined him at the sink, but before I could rearrange the plates, he slammed the dishwasher door shut and punched start. He disappeared into the bathroom and came back with his testosterone kit.

I laid out the materials—syringe, vial, alcohol wipe, Band-Aid—barely paying attention. I'd given Dillon his testosterone shots every fourteen days for years by this point.

Dillon lowered his jeans, and I wiped the target area with alcohol. The nurse had taught me to divide each buttock into quadrants and inject the top outer one, switching buttocks with each shot.

I said, "They're romanticizing a classist, colonial ideal and pretending to be English rich kids in the fin de siècle. Don't you find that problematic?"

"You're policing the hobbies of teens. You don't find *that* problematic?"

I drew oily testosterone from the glass vial into the syringe, then flicked it to get the air bubbles out. I inserted the needle into his skin, using the wrist motion the nurse had taught me. "Like throwing a dart," she'd said. I pulled the plunger out a little to see if I drew any blood, then slowly pushed the T into his flesh.

THAT NIGHT, WHILE Dillon snored beside me, I made a TikTok profile.

The algorithm gave me cat videos. I watched the cats for a reasonable amount of time. I liked cats, and I could no longer own one because of Dillon's allergies. Then I found my student Misty, dressed in a three-piece suit and sitting at a desk covered in papers. She chewed joylessly on the feather end of a quill while a voice-over read an Emily Dickinson poem.

Cut to Misty dipping the quill into an ink bottle.

Misty thoughtfully writing a letter.

Misty folding the letter like an Edwardian spinster and sealing it with melted wax and a custom metal stamp of her initials, *MOJ*. Her middle name was Ophelia, which she used as her online nom de plume.

When I looked up, it was two in the morning.

ON TUESDAY, I got a call from the doctor about Dorothy, my cyst. The doctor's voice was a gravelly tenor, confirming haltingly what the ultrasound technician had already said: a cyst the size of a golf ball on my left ovary.

"It might be precancerous," he said.

A small buzzing started in my ear. My manuscript, half-finished. Dillon, off on his second date.

"Nothing to worry about, maybe," the doctor said. "But all the same, we need to remove it."

When Dillon came back from his date, I stood in the bathroom doorway while he showered. I told him that Misty could actually be a good writer. She had the talent. But she was too busy playacting as a budget Oscar Wilde to actually write anything.

"You need to care less," Dillon said.

"All my students, really. They pretend to write hand-sealed letters to each other, but their essays and stories for class? Late, if they ever turn them in."

Dillon toweled off, and I rubbed lotion on his back.

"Seems like you're just upset that they've turned your livelihood into a performance," he said.

"They claim to love learning, but only for the likes."

I WAITED UNTIL Dillon was asleep, then made my first video on TikTok. It was all of one line, shot with terrible messy hair after a shower and a couple of glasses of wine: "Is dark academia just sad, burned-out gifted kids pretending to be English professors? Yes, yes I think so."

When I woke up in the middle of the night to pee, I checked my phone and saw a flurry of notifications. "LezBro02 and 49 others like your video," followed by individual notifications for a dozen comments.

The comments were a mix. Some took my jab lightly, exaggerating that they felt called out. Others wanted to fight me. I clicked "like" on a few comments that agreed with me. I replied with heart emojis for the users that thanked me for posting. But LezBro02 told me that I was just jealous, and it was this user I wanted to convince. It somehow felt intimate, both of us up in the wee hours of the morning, having a private conversation in public. After thirteen back-and-forth comments, LezBro02 called me a "poser bitch" and stopped responding.

ALL THROUGH THE day after, though I was running low on sleep and patience, I checked my comments on the video in between classes, meetings, and office hours. By midafternoon, I'd accumulated over two hundred likes and fifty comments, some of which talked about how "unaesthetic" my video was.

Misty sent me an email: *Dr. B! Saw the video! I know you didn't ask, but if you thought a little more about lighting and composition, you could really be killing it.*

I hurried home after my classes. Dillon wouldn't be out of work for at least a few more hours. I showered and put on makeup, clipped my hair up, and wore a silk blouse. I arranged myself in front of my bookshelves, turned the reading light toward my face, and shot another video, this one about how dark academia romanticized the British Empire's imperialism during the early twentieth century. I suggested that maybe Eurocentrism was a little too racist for our time.

I waited, refreshing my notifications after I posted. The views climbed. The comments flooded in. I liked and responded all through Dillon's arrival home, our take-out dinner, our settling into bed. By midnight, six hundred likes. Two hundred comments. Most of them were angry teenagers asking why they couldn't just like something, why I had to ruin their fun, why I was overthinking it all. But in between those comments, others praised me for finally saying it, for articulating the discomfort they could not find words for.

When Dillon rolled over to my side of the bed, something he did every day just before he woke, I was still up, still responding, embroiled in another comment war with LezBro02. I had hit three thousand likes.

"How long have you been up?" Dillon asked, blinking in the sunlight that rushed into our room. "Did you sleep at all?"

"I slept a little," I said, not taking my eyes off my phone.

My editor sent me an email asking when I'd have my revisions done for the poetry manuscript, and another email telling me about a social media workshop the press was running for writers. TikTok was the only marketing I needed, the email told me.

Dillon hugged my knees where I had drawn them close to me, and only then did I notice how stiff I was from hours of sitting in the same position. I stretched out. Dillon pried the phone from my hands and put it on the nightstand.

"Come cuddle with me," he said.

I scooted down and lay in bed with him.

"I have three thousand likes."

Dillon nuzzled his face into my shoulder, his new baby beard scratching me. "That sounds like a lot."

"Are you sure you want to keep the beard?"

It was patchy and made him look like a fifteen-year-old boy. I missed his smooth face.

"It helps me pass," he said, rubbing his bearded chin back and forth on my clavicle.

I scratched at the itch.

"I know, I know. It'll fill in."

I drew him close and smelled his neck, still warm and tinged with sweat and saliva from where he'd drooled a little in his sleep. I pulsed my abdominal muscles, hoping to feel Dorothy, to just have the steadiness of her presence. Nothing. I felt that desperation again and squeezed Dillon tight.

THE DOCTOR'S OFFICE kept calling me, trying to set up an appointment. I put a note on my to-do list: *call doctor back*. But every time I picked up the phone, TikTok suggested a new video or sent me my newest comments.

In the middle of class, while my students were writing on a prompt I'd given, I had three new ideas for videos. After class, I filmed them in my office, but during the editing, I realized that Misty was right. My office was sparse, ugly even, nothing like what other TikTok influencers had in their backgrounds. But I couldn't just film all the videos at home. I emailed Misty, and she showed up to office hours.

"How would you decorate this office?" I asked her. "I'm going to finally do it. I'm finally decorating."

Misty gasped and clapped her hands like a five-year-old seeing ice cream. "I have ideas."

Another student came to see me for office hours,

but I told him I needed to reschedule. Misty and I spent the next forty minutes buying decor online and setting it up for next-day delivery to the English Department.

I DIDN'T HAVE class or office hours the next day. I brought three boxes of my books from home to my university office, including all my leather- and cloth-bound ones. I hung string lights. I draped one of my mother's old dupattas like a tapestry. When I was done, I put on lipstick and a necklace and refilmed my three videos, changing out my jewelry and shirt each time.

Not long after I posted the first one, Misty sent me an email: *I saw the video. Wow, Dr. B, you're blowing my mind! Be sure to caption and subtitle and use a super popular bit of music as your background, even if you turn the volume way down. The algorithm likes that. And only post at the highest traffic hours.*

My video was about the actual meaning of the word *aesthetic*, before the internet created a new meaning by misusing it. Again, furious arguments raged in the comments. As I scrolled, TikTok suggested I watch a video of a masculine lesbian, ball cap on backward so a tuft of blond hair peeked from the opening, who licked her lips suggestively at the camera. That was it. Five seconds of her licking her lips and looking at the camera like she wanted to fuck whoever was on the other end. She had four times as many views as all of my videos combined.

LezBro02 commented on my new post: *Why can't you leave us alone you old cunt!*

I LOOKED UP the highest traffic hours for TikTok, then waited to post the next video until Dillon went out for his second date with New Cologne. I did what Misty had suggested. I spent twenty minutes captioning, using hashtags, and picking out background music from the stuff that was already going viral.

I left my phone facedown on the kitchen counter for the first few minutes after posting. I walked through the house. I forced myself to not pick it up, watching the clock on the microwave instead, waiting for it to tick three more minutes before I allowed myself the phone.

Thirty likes. Not nearly enough. I put the phone down again, thought about weeding the garden, then decided against it. I popped a beer and made myself some ramen, the unhealthy kind that Dillon always made a fuss about. I added two heaping teaspoons of cayenne pepper, two more of curry powder, a dash of chili oil, and a generous squirt of sriracha and set the pot to simmer so that the noodles could soak up as much of the liquid as possible.

I captioned my next video. I had five thousand followers. The comments section was still heated, with a few even posting reaction videos. One person stitched my video with their own, emphatically nodding along to everything I said. Another told me I was overreaching, looking for problems with dark academia that weren't there.

TikTok suggested another video of a masculine lesbian, this one refurbishing an antique birthing chair.

I watched it, entranced, and hit "like." Immediately, TikTok suggested ten more videos to watch.

The ramen burned to the bottom of the pot. I ate it on the porch, scraping the now-crispy noodles where they'd congealed to the pot, watching as many TikTok videos of masc lesbians as the algorithm would feed me. Afterward, I masturbated to the original video of the woman licking her lips at the camera and slept for an hour.

When Dillon finally came home, giggling and tipsy, I woke up and checked the phone. Six thousand followers and counting. I posted the third video while he showered, then managed to not check the phone while he climbed into bed. He rolled over to sleep, but I stayed up, watching the comments roll in. My latest video was about the actual meaning of the term *academia*. LezBro02 was incensed, commenting, *Why don't you climb out of that ivory tower and get your head out of your own ass?*

For the rest of the night, I stayed awake while TikTok fed me a string of videos. Around three in the morning, a theme emerged: lesbians complaining about being afraid to date bisexual and pansexual women, how bi and pan women would always leave you for a man. Several asked, *Are bisexuals even real?*

DESPITE TWO CUPS of strong coffee the next Monday, I was too tired to teach. I emailed my three classes that I wasn't feeling well and told them to take a workday. At home, still in my fuzzy slippers, I carefully picked out three outfits, matching jewelry, and makeup. I filmed three videos entitled "Dear Lesbian TikTok," in which I fast-cut shots of me drinking tea, posing glamorously, and waving. Each video was less than ten seconds long—which was good for the algorithm—and tried to communicate only one simple thought. No narration. Only text.

The first video said, simply: *the gender of our partners does not negate or define our bisexuality.*

I posted and set the phone down on the kitchen counter. Almost immediately, a notification badge popped up on the lock screen. I took a breath.

As I reached for the phone, the doctor's office called. I watched it ring.

I tried to feel Dorothy. Nothing, just like before. But Dorothy was there, inside me, the size of a golf ball. Growing like a little baby.

The phone continued to ring, oblivious to the gathering TikTok notifications, one for each comment, the likes grouped in stacks of fifty. I waited. The ringtone stopped. The notifications continued. Already, two hundred likes. I opened the app and sat down in a dining chair.

A bloodbath unfolded on my screen. LezBro02 had responded a few seconds after I posted: *Are you a lesbian? If not, you have no right to talk to the community.* Others had joined in. Many others. So many that my comments were mostly angry screaming in all caps. *LEAVE US ALONE! THIS IS LESBOPHOBIA! BISEXUALS LIKE YOU ARE ALWAYS TRYING TO TAKE OVER OUR COMMUNITIES! NO BISEXUALS ALLOWED ON LESBIAN TIKTOK!!!!*

I sat, stunned. I hadn't encountered that level

of biphobic assholery since the early aughts. I'd thought we were beyond it as a culture. I scrolled through, looking to see if Misty had liked or responded to this video. She'd once told me during introductions in my queer lit class that she, too, was bisexual.

The doctor's office called again, lighting up my screen. My head, body, hands, fingers—all buzzed independently of the phone. LezBro02 made another comment: *I bet you're not even a lesbian you fake!*

I answered the phone.

"We've been trying to reach you," the receptionist said. Her voice reminded me of a TikTok influencer I'd been following who dressed in Regency garb and dropped little-known facts about gender and sexual fluidity in European history.

"Sorry," I said. "I had work."

"We have the results of your ultrasound. You need to come in to consult with the doctor."

My whole body thrummed with vibration, like I was the one ringing with a call.

"Can you come in tomorrow at three P.M.? Hello? Are you there?"

"I'm here."

"Tomorrow at three P.M.?"

I lifted my phone from my cheek, and already there were more comments to read and respond to.

"Hello? Ma'am?"

"Yes, tomorrow at three P.M."

THE DOCTOR'S OFFICE smelled like antiseptic and figs. Cheery-blue walls with a desk and three chairs, two on one side, one on the other. A giant bulletin board crammed with pictures of all the babies that, presumably, had been delivered by this doctor.

I sat alone in the office after the nurse showed me in, scrolling through the comments on my new video. I'd posted it just before getting into the car to come to the office. This one said, *Dear Lesbian TikTok: bisexuals have been part of lesbian communities for a long, long time.*

More angry, all-caps screaming in the comments.

DON'T TRESPASS ON OUR SPACES! LIES LIES LIES! WHAT MAKES YOU SUCH AN EXPERT? ARE YOU A LESBIAN? TELL US!

I imagined Dorothy inside me, incensed at these kids for attacking one of their own, for not knowing their own history. But I still couldn't feel her.

A new comment from LezBro02: *Check out the Lesbian Masterdoc for a real history lesson you dumb fuck.*

Misty emailed me: *You're sure stirring the pot, Dr. B.*

I googled "Lesbian Masterdoc." I did teach queer studies, after all. I should be informed.

The Lesbian Masterdoc was a Google Doc from a 2018 Tumblr page, passed around on hundreds of Reddit threads and linked to on thousands of TikTok videos. As I read, the world around me narrowed to the buzzing inside me. The world was the phone, the lies it held, the utter sadness that a whole generation of queer people were living with no awareness of their own histories, that they were learning about queerness from a viral document that read like it was written by a nineteen-year-old who'd only half paid attention in Introduction to Women and Gender Studies. In its bibliography, the doc only cited other Tumblr pages.

The Lesbian Masterdoc asked the question, "Are you a lesbian?" and then provided the answer "yes," ignoring any idea of pan or bisexuality. You were attracted to men, it said, only because you've been indoctrinated by compulsory heterosexuality.

I reedited what was supposed to be my next video. I'd been planning to talk about toxic masculinity in the lesbian community, but I deleted the text captions and started over. As I was typing, the doctor came in.

He was a kind-looking man with thin gray eyebrows on a dark face that made it look like someone had carved half-moon arches over his eyes.

"It's not great news," he said. "But don't freak out."

I was still holding my phone, the cursor blinking.

The doctor walked by the bulletin board, noticed

a push-pinned picture that was slightly askew, and righted it. He adjusted his white coat, standing behind his desk.

"You have a cyst," he said. His voice was casual. "We don't know if it's benign or cancerous, but it's safe to assume this is precancer."

He whipped out a pen from his pocket, uncapped it with an air of ceremony, and drew a picture for me. A line, divided. On the left, the stages of precancer. On the right, the stages of cancer.

"You're probably here," he said, pointing close to the demarcated line between precancer and actual cancer. "But we won't know for sure until we biopsy it. We'll need to remove it, of course."

"Of course." I glanced down at the phone. The cursor blinked. I had thirty-one more comments since the last time I'd looked. Plus a text from Dillon: *Date night tonight? Just the two of us?*

"We had a cancellation next Monday," the doctor said. "Are you good with that date?"

"I have to teach," I said.

The doctor pinched the bridge of his nose with his stemlike fingers.

"Can you cancel classes? We don't have any other openings for over a month, and I don't think we should wait that long."

That humming inside me, a low simmer.

"Monday?" the doctor asked again. He looked at me with those half-moon arches over his eyes. "We need to get that thing out of you."

I POSTED THE next video with a single line: *the Lesbian Masterdoc is bisexual erasure.* I watched the progress line on my screen fill up. As soon as it completed, the usual notifications began. The bubbles stacked on top of one another, pushing the others down into the abyss of the screen's edge.

The door opened, and Dillon came in, damp from the rain outside.

"Ready for date night?" he asked, too chipper.

I showed him my phone screen, alive with notification boxes pushing one another out of the way.

"Your three thousand followers?" He shook out his hair like a dog, droplets flying everywhere. One single drop hung on the edge of his eyebrow.

"It's twelve thousand now."

MY BODY AND phone hummed all through cocktails, appetizers, wine, dinner, and dessert at our favorite Italian restaurant that was so loud we had to shout to hear each other. A constant buzzing in my purse. I'd turned on the vibrations for TikTok notifications. Dillon looked at my purse every few minutes until I put it underneath our table.

My hands itched. The lamb chops I'd eaten sat in my stomach like a mass, pulling me to the ground. The restaurant itself was dim and looked like the inside of a Restoration Hardware store. Misty worked here, or so she'd told me.

"Stop jiggling your leg," Dillon said. He put a hand on my knee where I kept pumping it up and down. "Please."

The phone kept vibrating at my ankle, with a little

metallic sound added as it moved around in my purse toward my keys.

"You need to detox from your phone, baby," Dillon said. "It's not healthy."

"Drinking two cocktails and then sharing a bottle of wine isn't healthy," I said, "but here we are." I wondered if LezBro02 had responded yet, what kinds of things were happening in the comments section that I wasn't seeing. If I didn't respond to comments fast enough, the algorithm would stop pushing my content.

"Dr. B?"

It was Misty, her hair pulled back into a sleek high ponytail, dressed in black trousers and a white shirt. She ambled over, a giant plastic tub in her hands.

"You're blowing up," she said. She reached for my empty dessert plate and put it in her tub.

"Did you see the last video?" I asked.

Her eyes flicked to Dillon, then back to me. "They're calling you a fraud."

"A fraud?" Dillon looked back and forth between us. "For what?"

Misty's eyes roved over Dillon. I wondered how old he looked to her, if she was clocking his patchy beard and adolescent voice, if she knew what the signs meant.

"That you're not a real lesbian," Misty said.

"I'm not." I watched Misty's face closely, but it stayed frozen. "But that doesn't mean what I said isn't true."

Misty sloshed the water around in her plastic tub. "Of course, Dr. B. I didn't mean—I think you're right. But you stirred the pot. The pot's full of wasps."

My phone continued to vibrate in my purse. I pressed the side of my foot against it, letting the humming reach into my bones. I imagined Dorothy waking from her slumber, wondered if she'd coo in support or roar in fury.

"I said what needed to be said."

"What did you say?" Dillon asked.

Misty held the tub on her hip as if it were a baby. "Dr. B attacked the Masterdoc. If there's one rule of lesbian TikTok, it's 'don't attack the Masterdoc.'"

"What the hell is the Masterdoc?"

If I didn't know, I'd have assumed from the way they were talking that the Masterdoc was the big bad monster in an alien movie, some sort of mother queen the rest of the hive served obediently.

The image wormed a laugh out of me, a laugh that wouldn't stop. I bent over my crumpled napkin, laughing until I coughed.

"Fuck the Masterdoc," I said.

Misty shifted the tub to her other hip. "Dr. B," she said, "you're the one who taught me to not expect nuance from the internet. You told me that's why you don't do social media, remember?"

It sounded like something I would say, but I couldn't remember saying it.

"Besides," Misty said, "the Masterdoc has helped a lot of people realize they really are lesbians. It's not fair of you to attack that experience just because you don't agree with it."

"Aren't you bisexual, though?" I asked.

Dillon put his hand over mine on the table.

"I don't know anymore, Dr. B," Misty said. She dipped her finger in the dirty tub water and then flicked it off. "A lot of us are still figuring it out."

"And I'm not? Look at me, I look straight to everyone now!"

Dillon flinched.

"Do you agree with them, Misty? You think I'm not allowed to talk about lesbians because I'm not one?"

Misty's sneakers squeaked as she shifted her weight.

"Well?"

"Baby," Dillon said.

"Well?" I asked.

Misty turned and walked away. As she wove through the tables, she clipped her tub against a table, and a wine glass crashed to the floor. Misty dropped to her knees to pick up the pieces.

I took stock of the emotions vying for attention inside me, trying to see if guilt was among them. I started to get up to help her, then sat back down.

Regardless of any merits of the Masterdoc, it still erased the experiences of anyone who was genuinely attracted to multiple genders.

I managed to wait until Misty went through the kitchen door. Then I retrieved my purse.

"Are you serious?" Dillon said.

"I need to see." I pulled out the phone. The video had garnered sixteen thousand views, two thousand comments, and fifty-two video responses.

"Why do you even care about the comments?" Dillon asked on the drive home.

I ignored him. I wanted to type furious, indignant responses. Scholarly responses explaining the nuances of bisexual erasure. I composed them in my head, but there were too many comments now. I couldn't respond to them individually. I had to make a new video.

WHEN WE GOT home, I slammed through the doorway and went upstairs, already composing the new video in my head. I propped my phone into the tripod I'd bought.

Before I could start recording, Dillon crossed the length of the office and snatched the tripod away. He pushed his own phone into my hand. "Look at this. Just look."

On the screen of his phone was the only picture I'd allowed him to post of us on our wedding day, only it had been posted on Twitter by a stranger, with my TikTok profile linked and Dillon tagged. The caption read, *Queer my ass. You're a straight bitch and we all know.* Underneath the tweet, comments were stacking up.

"I'm connected to this now," Dillon said. He slowly sank into an office chair, still holding the tripod out of my reach. "I didn't know you were getting all this hate. Why didn't you tell me?"

His phone vibrated with notifications now, too. They had found him not just on Twitter but on Facebook and Instagram. LezBro02 had sent him a direct message: *How does it feel to know your wife just wants to eat pussy?*

"Just give me my phone," I said. "I need to make

another video. I need to tell them this kind of harassment isn't okay."

Dillon stared at me for a few seconds before his face broke in anger. "Do you hear yourself? A video isn't going to fix this!" He seized both phones away from my grasp. His eyes roamed over the screens. "Holy shit. Shit. Fuck."

He showed me. On his Twitter notifications, a post by LezBro02: *Looks like they're both lesbians after all.* Attached was our wedding photo and a picture of Dillon pretransition, in a sports bra and swim shorts at the beach.

With his beautiful shoulders slumped, Dillon handed my phone and tripod back to me. Already, dozens of notifications had accumulated. I opened TikTok. LezBro02 had posted the same pictures in a video stitched with mine. Comments screamed underneath. *DON'T YOU KNOW SEX IS A BIOLOGICAL FACT!! THINKING YOU'RE A MAN IS A MENTAL ILLNESS! WOMEN PRETENDING TO BE MEN ARE TRAITORS TO THE CAUSE!!!*

"I'm blocking them and shutting this all down," Dillon said. He squinted in concentration, clutching his phone in his lap. "You should do the same."

"Running away is not the answer," I said. There was fire inside me, a constant IV drip of adrenaline that told me to fight. Maybe this was Dorothy's fault. Dorothy the cyst was feeding me combat hormones.

Dillon was silent, hunched over his phone. "Block them all," he muttered. "Shut it down."

I clicked "reply" to LezBro02's video. The cursor blinked. The flames inside me licked at my chest. Before I could harness my thoughts enough to type, my phone rang. My department chair.

"Sorry to call so late," my department chair said. "This couldn't wait. I got the email just now, and I wanted to give you a heads up of the procedure moving forward."

"Procedure? What email?"

Dillon's head clipped up, listening.

"Yes, yes," my department chair said. "I got an

email from one of your students. Misty Johnson. She's lodged a formal complaint against you."

"Misty?" My head swirled, incoherent.

"She says that you were demeaning to her and that you belittled her and called her a child."

"I did not."

"And that you did so in public. At a restaurant, while she was working."

"We just had a discussion!"

"We'll get an independent investigator, but until then, you're not to have any contact with the student."

"It was a discussion pertaining to course-related queer issues."

"She won't be required to attend your classes. You must provide all relevant materials to her, and I'll be grading her assignments myself."

I hung up before my chair could say goodbye.

"You heard all that?" I asked Dillon.

Instead of answering, Dillon hugged me, pulling me to the carpet. "You didn't call Misty a child," he said.

My phone lit up with more notifications. One video caught my eye. A new one that I was tagged in. I squirmed out of Dillon's hold and clicked "open."

LezBro02 had posted a picture of our house, with our address superimposed. Now every wasp in the pot knew exactly where we lived. The world stilled around us, squeezing out everything else except the two of us on the floor and the house on the screen. The seconds ticked by. Then Dillon went for his phone and started scrolling.

"It's on Twitter," he said. "And Facebook. And Instagram. And Reddit. They've tagged me."

I sat on the floor, the world thrumming with a drumbeat I couldn't quite hear.

"We have to get out of here," Dillon said.

When I didn't move, he pulled me forcefully to a standing position. I followed him in a haze to our bedroom, where he took down a duffle bag from the closet and threw clothes into it. He disappeared into the bathroom and came back with our toothbrushes, which he flung on top of the clothes. He zipped up the bag, took me by the hand, and led me out to the car.

I SAT IN silence, watching the screen of my phone, as Dillon drove.

"Are you listening to me?" Dillon's voice was rising in volume, drowning out even the phone's vibrations at each new comment.

"It's Misty," I said. "It's got to be. How would anyone know our house? Or that you're my partner? It's Misty." I wanted to spit, to punch and kick and wail. "She's LezBro02."

"That sounds like a conspiracy theory. She wouldn't do something like this, would she?"

"It could be her."

"Could. Probably isn't."

I wanted to hurt him. I tensed my abdomen, a last plea to Dorothy to show herself. She was pumping me full of fire, but I wanted to feel her.

"I have to get a precancerous cyst removed on Monday," I said.

Dillon turned fully to look at me. "What?"

"Don't get into an accident."

He spun back to the road, his fingers clamped tight around the steering wheel.

"What do you mean, a precancerous cyst?"

"It's not a big deal. I don't want to talk about it."

Dillon swerved onto the shoulder.

"We're on the highway!"

He braked the car to a stop. "What the hell?" he said. "What cyst? How long have you known? Why didn't you tell me?"

The phone dinged and dinged with more notifications.

"Are you seriously looking at your phone right now?" he yelled.

A new comment from LezBro02: *Biological sex is real and unchangeable.*

"These transphobic idiots don't know anything about biology," I said.

Another comment from LezBro02: *You're just another patriarchal oppressor.*

I screamed in frustration.

Dillon grabbed the phone out of my hand. He rolled the window down on his side and threw it out, onto the dark highway.

"What the fuck!"

I opened the door.

"Wait," Dillon said. But I was already out of the car, hurrying around it to get to my phone.

I looked left down the dark road. A pair of headlights closed in, barreling forward in the lane where my phone had probably landed. I took a step into the road. The phone dinged, the screen lighting up a few feet in front of me. The headlights drew closer.

I started to take another step, but then Dillon's arms closed around me, pulling me back. The car honked loudly as it sped past, its tailwind whipping us together. I squirmed in Dillon's grip, fighting.

He let me go. I whirled, searching for the glow of the screen, but there was nothing. Just black asphalt. No phone. Silence.

I pounded my fists on Dillon's chest, but he caught

them. He held my wrists tightly, raising them above my head and pinning them to the side of our car. My whole body went weak, as if all the electricity in my cells had discharged and I was now a blown fuse.

Dillon threw open the door to the back seat and tossed me inside. Despite his agitated state, he was careful not to hit my head on the doorframe. I started to get wet at the pressure of Dillon's body against mine, the sheer strength with which he'd lifted me. I held his shoulders tightly as he tried to let go.

"I need you all to myself," I said.

Both driver-side doors hung open as cars whizzed past, some of them laying on their horns.

Dillon lunged at my neck, biting hard. Two fingers went up my skirt, pulled my underwear to the side, and slipped into me. As he pumped his fingers in and out, almost raising me from the seat and surely bruising my labia, I felt her. Finally. Dorothy stabbed me with pain like a tiny knife, focused and sharp, right where I'd thought she'd been all this time. Pleasure and pain blurred in that hot night air, swirling up inside me like a double helix. Dillon and Dorothy. Dorothy and Dillon. My whole body vibrated like a tuning fork, as if it were the last moment I'd be held together, as if afterward I'd just dissolve.

In the flashing lights of an approaching police car, as we gathered our clothes around us, I saw it—my phone, still in the road, still dinging with notifications.

PATRIOTS' DAY

Four days before his death, Amit Srinivasan files for divorce. He's living in a tiny apartment in Somerville that he began renting in December, ever since his wife packed a suitcase full of his clothes and burned it in the backyard firepit of their suburban brick house. Winter has broken, and Somerville's tree-lined streets rupture with color. Pink petals work their way into the cracked, uneven sidewalks.

As soon as Amit files for divorce, he calls Hannah. She doesn't pick up. He leaves her a voice mail. "We can be together now," he says. "I love you," he says. "I filed for divorce," he says. But four days pass, and Hannah doesn't call back.

At 8:10 P.M. on April 15, a woman named Pamela

Robertson will push Amit in front of an orange-line train at the Forest Hills T stop in Boston. She will be frustrated, and all it'll take is a little shove, a couple pounds of pressure. Amit will already be over the line, standing with his toes butting into the yellow markings on the platform. He will be leaning forward, looking into the tunnel as the headlights fill the empty stone void, the light rushing closer, and Pamela will put out her arm and shove him in the back, her fingernails scraping against his trench coat, and he will hang there, slanted, poised between death and the platform. Pamela will be able to picture it, years later, the way his body will hang diagonal between the platform and the yellow line, the way the tunnel will fill with light, the way the rumbling train will carry him off like a leaf.

When police officers ask her why she did it, she won't tell them. Pamela will feel her skin, the clothes over them, the air around her and the officers. This is what she will know: that she has a chip in one of her nails from the blending machine she operates at Toni's Chocolate Factory; that there are 1.82 ounces of white chocolate in each almond macaroon they make; that she needs her roots touched up where the gray is starting to shine; that her appointment is on April 16 at 4 P.M. with Amanda; that she is wearing the wrong type of shoes; that for her flat feet, she should really wear sneakers when she stands at the machines all day, but she can't bring herself to give up her polished-leather penny loafers like her mother used to wear.

On the morning of his death, Amit heaves himself out of bed and turns on the TV in his tiny Somerville apartment. The red line rumbles beneath the floorboards.

He looks around and thinks that he needs to get a clock. He could get some plants, or a picture frame to hang over the white spot on the wall where someone patched over a hole and neglected to paint it. He could make a home here. He could be happy. He could take his kids to Boston on the weekends, buy them food in Chinatown, watch all the parades and shows they missed before, back when the thought of driving to Boston on the weekends exhausted him.

But his wife won't let him see their children anymore. She claims his affair with Hannah is a bad influence, that therefore *he* is a bad influence, a bad father, a bad husband, and a bad man. His wife often thinks in absolutes. She likes the stratifications of ordinary things: poverty and wealth, piety and sin, love and divorce. Amit knows he will have to sue for partial custody, that the judge will ask if he has enough space in his apartment to house his kids, that he'll have to say no, that he'll only be allowed a day or two with them a week.

Amit wants to sink down into the weary mattress springs, down through the floorboards and into the earth. He wonders how things went so wrong. Something had burned off his childhood optimism like fog in the sun.

He and Hannah fought viciously the last time he saw her, their biggest fight in the two years they'd been dating. "Do you love me like you loved your wife?" That was the question. A trick question, he has since realized. A question to which "First love only happens once" was the wrong answer. Hannah hasn't talked to her mother for three years because they disagreed over her father's funeral arrangements, something about who got to give eulogies and which flowers were placed next to the casket. He knows Hannah can hold a grudge.

Amit reheats the naan and palak paneer left over from his take-out dinner at the Indian place down the street. The palak paneer tastes like the Styrofoam container he heated it in, but he eats it anyway.

ON APRIL 15, Pamela calls her daughter Hannah before work. She calls her daughter every day before work, though Hannah hasn't picked up for over three years. Pamela says the same thing into the voice mail that she does every day: "I miss you. Call me. Your father and I love you." Pamela's husband has been dead three and a half years. Heart attack. Her daughter walked out of the funeral and hasn't spoken to her since.

Pamela wraps her green paisley scarf around her neck, slips her feet into her shiny leather penny loafers, and steps outside. She makes sure to lock the dead bolt on her apartment door. She walks down the stairs of her condo building, her knees creaking with every step. Maybe it's time to move, she thinks. Maybe she should get a nice house without stairs, somewhere outside of town. Newton. Concord, even. Go north. Away from the bustle of the city, north to the sleepy towns where locals in costume still reenact the start of the American Revolution. What would she do in such a town? She's so used to the T that she knows most schedules by heart. Her feet carry her to where she needs to go, without having to think about Boston's winding streets. She likes the chaos, likes that people who have lived in Boston for all their lives can still get lost, likes that she never does.

AMIT DRESSES AND walks down to the coffee shop on his block. Five dollars for a latte. He can't keep that up, not if he's going to pay rent and half a mortgage. Two dollars for a coffee. Better. Back then, his wife blamed their money problems on his one-bottle-of-whiskey-a-week habit, on his SUV, on his budgetless trips to Toys "R" Us. In turn, he blamed his wife's collection of shoes stuffed into the hall closet, her Coach bags, her weekly manicures and monthly facials. Back then, he was careful to never take home the restaurant receipts, the bar tabs, the mini hotel shampoos.

At CVS, he buys a pack of Marlboro Lights. He's never been a regular smoker, but it feels good to have something in between his fingers, ashes to flick to the ground. Outside the Davis Square T station, he asks a stranger for a light, and the man steps so close to light it for him that, for a moment, standing in the haze of the man's cologne, Amit feels a shock up and down his body. He hasn't been so close to another human in days, not since he last saw Hannah.

He had met Hannah at the pool, where they both swam at the same time after work. Back when he used to swim, back when he thought he could make his wife happy if only he looked better or spoke better or bought her flowers. But by then, it was too late. Suspicion had grown like a monster in his wife's head, had sprung from her imagination before he had even thought of other women. The night he met Hannah, he came home to find his wife on the floor of their kitchen, cradling some roses he had brought home for her the night before. Her constant accusations had made him feel like a cheater long before he committed anything worthy of her suspicion.

PAMELA ROBERTSON TAKES the T to the chocolate factory in Somerville. She stands pressed up against young students with backpacks. College students perhaps, but she can't tell anymore, not like she could when her daughter was in school. Back then, she could pinpoint their ages like cities on a map. Hannah's age. A year older. Two years younger. But now she barely notices them and doesn't care for their blank-faced ages. Fodder for the cubicle farms. Not her. No, thank you. Pamela likes the chocolate factory with its smells and the white coveralls the employees have to wear. Macaroons, cupcakes, truffles—what they make changes by the day. Always something new. Some new taste. Some new ingredient.

Her friend Ellen is waiting for her at the door like she always does, primping her silver curls and watching her reflection in the tinted glass. In the locker rooms, they put their purses in identical, eye-height lockers and get white coveralls out of the laundry bin. Pamela can never figure out how the laundry workers get all those chocolate stains out, but every morning, the coveralls are there, as pristine as if they'd just been sewn.

AMIT LIKES THE way you can see end to end on a green-line train, the way the cars snake through corners, wrapping around each bend like a time warp.

A cop stands in every T car, not holding on to

anything. People flow and jostle around the officers, talking loudly about the marathon.

Somerville was warm, but Boston is exceptionally windy. Amit comes up the steps, and the wind reaches into the tunnels. Copley Station is closed for the marathon, so he gets off at Arlington and walks. Boylston Street bursts with chaos. People are already lining up at the finish line, their faces painted, their bodies bundled against the wind. Barriers close off the road to traffic.

More cops stand along both sides of Boylston. The wind blows at their coats, knocks down trash bins, rolls empty plastic bottles all over the streets. Pigeons peck near their feet. But still the cops stand in their navy and silver.

PAMELA CLOCKS IN at 8:47 A.M. She and Ellen work the same station, which today is a new biscotti recipe. Amaretto. Which means a smell that Pamela doesn't care for. She likes the aromas of melting sugar, chopped nuts, chocolate, fruit. But amaretto burns her nostrils in a way that reminds her of her late husband and his liquor cabinet.

The station manager is a woman half Pamela's age, a woman who, Pamela knows, started at the factory ten years after Pamela and five years after Ellen.

Heather the station manager sneers over her clipboard. She has lipstick on her teeth, a garish shade of pink that Pamela would never wear. Prostitute pink. Maybe Heather's trying to catch the eye of the foreman. He's always lusting after one or more of the workers. If that's it, then Heather has some stiff competition. She's over thirty and looks older, with a belly that's starting to hang over the elastic waist of her white suit.

"New recipe today, girls," Heather says. False cheer. Drawn-on eyebrows. "Amaretto biscotti. This one's going to be big. Corporate thinks it's going to be big."

Pamela tries to catch Ellen's eye. They had both been there when corporate thought chocolate bacon

SJ SINDU

was going to be big, then walnut-crusted mints after that. As far as Pamela's concerned, corporate is full of young ninnies who would never buy the factory's chocolates if they saw them in a grocery store.

There was a time when Pamela thought she could be one of them, when she wanted to try to work her way up the company and into a corner office. She was young. She knows now that no one makes it from the factory floor to corporate. Those offices are full of people who have never worn white coveralls. And so Pamela decided she likes the factory floor. It's more honest, this working with flour and sugar and shaping sweets out of thin air.

Heather passes out copies of the recipe and gives them assignments. Ellen on flour and sugar, Pamela on amaretto.

AMIT'S OFFICE IS empty, even though it's Monday. Everyone with a salary stays home on marathon day. The only workers who show up are hourly temps and their managers.

At his desk, Amit puts down his things and gets himself a coffee. Thirteen unread emails. A call from Kate in reception: "Your herd of new temps is ready." He goes down to the lobby. He has to remember to call Veronica at the temp agency. Who tells temps to start on marathon day?

A group of young white women stand against the metal logo on the wall, looking lonely and lost. One of them has his wife's round face. One has her jagged, sawed-off jaw. One is wearing her hair in curls the way his wife does on special occasions. They stare at him but don't hold his eye contact, like he's translucent, like they can see through him down to his dark insides, like they can see the blood in his veins, like they suspect it isn't red, like they want to test the theory. This divorce must be weighing on him more than he realizes if he's seeing his wife everywhere in the faces of others. His mother told him to always see God inside others. He tries. He tries to imagine a warm ball of light inside each of the new temps. Little balls of light they are, all gathered around him in this lobby.

"Good morning," he says. "How is everyone today?"

The women—girls, really—look at each other. They look at the floor. They look back at Kate the receptionist.

One girl, mousy and pale, says "Good morning" back. She introduces herself. The others mumble their names. Amit leads them on a tour of the building. Whenever he turns his back, he can feel their eyes on him, crawling like bugs, all over, everywhere. He points out the women's bathroom, the cafeteria on the ninth floor that looks out onto Copley Square, the showers on the tenth, the kitchenettes tucked into the corners where people put food left over from meetings.

"The first rule of proofreading," he says, "is to always let your co-workers know when there's free food."

He waits for them to laugh. After a few seconds, a couple of them smile nervously. He's off his game today. He shows them to their cubicles, but their computer log-ins don't work. He walks them to the front of the building, where, through the floor-to-ceiling windows, they can see the marathoners pass by. Hordes of spectators push at one another on the sidewalks. The temps flatten their faces against the glass and watch.

An hour passes, and the IT techs—mediocre Indian-educated men the company imports because they're cheaper than the made-in-the-USA models—have no idea when the temps will be able to log in. Amit still remembers the programs he wrote as a high schooler, the days he spent dreaming about being the next Silicon Valley tycoon. But then in college, he took that philosophy class, that damn philosophy class, and suddenly he thought he understood his parents and the rift that had formed between them and his brothers. The only thing he really understood at the end of it all was the real tragedy of immigration: that it made parents and children strangers to one another, created a cultural gap too wide to fill. If you stay on one side, you'll always yearn for the other. If you try to straddle the abyss, you'll fall.

The worst part of it is that his wife—born and raised in India—doesn't even understand him. Whatever she had expected in an American husband, he wasn't it. Ex-wife, he reminds himself. Almost.

Amit lets the temps take a three-hour lunch with a pile of board games while he fights with IT and swallows his blood pressure tablets. He tries to get work done but ends up thinking about Hannah. He checks his phone like a tic. Still nothing. They'd talked every day for two years, and now four days seems like she may never call again.

He tries to think of the temps, how smooth their faces are, how their innocence should excite him. At one point, he would have flirted with them. But now he feels tired. He no longer has the energy to chase girls half his age.

The internet is down. Amit's day normally consists of answering endless emails. Panicked project managers. Disgruntled copy editors who think proofreading is trying to do their jobs. Upper management, who keeps trying to move the proofreaders to another building in Arlington. IT, who wants to go paperless. Temp agencies with résumés from eager college grads. Everyone wants something. The temps want to be paid better. The permanent employees want vacation time. His wife wants him to be the man she thought he was when she married him. What does Amit want? Right now, he wants a beer from the bar down the street. He wants to erase Hannah from his mind, and he wants to be near her again. He wants his son and daughter to visit him in his apartment. He wants a bigger apartment. He wants to give each of them a room.

THE AMARETTO NEEDS to be fetched from the storage floor, where Carl the stock guy heaves it onto a cart with a smile. If she had time, Pamela would wait to see if he smiles at the next woman who shows up or if his smile is just for her.

Pamela wheels the cart down, taps the keg, and fixes it to the machine that pumps it into a measuring vat and from there into the kneading bucket. According to the recipe, the amaretto needs to be added while the dough is kneading. The siphon slowly pours a stream of brown liquid over the mass of dough.

The smell of amaretto turns her stomach, though she tries not to let that show on her face. If Heather assigned this to her on purpose, Pamela doesn't want to give her the satisfaction.

Pamela's husband loved amaretto sours, and she had made one for him every day when he came home from work. "I'm home, honey. Make me a drink, will you?" Sometimes when she opens the door to her condo after work, the walls say those same words to her. "Honey, I'm home. Make me a drink, will you?"

WHEN HE GOES to the temp cubicles after lunch, Amit finds the girls talking with one another. They stop when they see him. He feels their eyes on him again, itching all over.

"It seems like IT will be a while with your log-ins, so you can start with paper."

He shows them the wall of projects. They follow him like ducklings.

"Project managers drop off the manuscript." He takes one out to show them. Back when he was a proofreader, it was all paper, and he likes the weight of it in his hands. "Always go through the order form, then the cover sheet. You'll start with spot checks, then move up to first reads when you feel ready. Check corrections are the hardest."

A faraway sound—like a balloon popping—cuts him off. It echoes through the empty office.

The temps look around. Another pop. It came from the street. Amit walks to the windows that look out over Boylston. The crowd below wavers, grinds into itself like wheat in a mill. Muffled screams float up the seven floors.

The temps gather at the window.

"There," one says. She points down Boylston toward Copley Square and the finish line.

Something litters the ground a block down from the building. Bits of paper. Bits of banners. Red smeared over the concrete.

Amit steadies himself with a hand on the wall. Time warps around him, stretches itself out and scrunches back. He thinks of the green-line train. Sound cuts to silence, and he doesn't feel the minutes pass.

One of the temps has her phone out.

"They're saying it was a bomb," she says.

The word falls leaden onto the floor. Amit feels the room tilt for a just a moment. "How can you know that already?" he asks.

"It's on Twitter." Her hand scrapes at her chest. She's wheezing and looking around wildly.

Amit guides her back toward the center of the floor. He's grateful for something to do. Without the temps to herd, he thinks he'd be the stray one.

"Shouldn't we evacuate?" someone asks. "We need to leave."

"No," Amit says. "We're on the seventh floor of a stone building. We're safe." He believes himself.

He leads them to their cubicles, away from any windows.

The temps have phones out and are frantically typing. One looks up from her screen. "I've lost reception," she says.

"Me, too."

"Holy shit."

Amit left his phone at his desk. His hand tingles in its absence.

"Everyone stay here," he says. "No one move."

They stare at him blankly. A couple of girls pull air into their lungs as if they're drowning. A phone rings. He goes back to his desk. It's the landline.

"Hello?"

"Amit." Hannah's voice. The sound makes him feel solid again. "I couldn't get through on your cell. What's going on?"

"We don't know yet. We don't know."

"But you're okay."

"I'm okay. You're okay."

"They evacuated our building. I'm going home."

He remembers the red on the sidewalk. He grabs his stapler, a sea-green one that his wife got him as a birthday present. He should've known then. No one gives a stapler as a gift to a loved one. The stapler is scratched up now, the electroplated paint stripping away to reveal the dark metal underneath.

"Come see me," Hannah says. "Come over."

"Why didn't you call me before?"

"Just come."

PAMELA STANDS NEXT to Ellen, who's working the kneading machine. They watch the dull blades push and pull at the dough. After the kneading machine, the dough goes to the shaper, where it's made into wide, flat loaves to be baked. The loaves are as long as they can be while still being able to support their own weight once baked.

Break time. Pamela and Ellen go down to the cafeteria. They get tea and sit themselves down at one of the indoor picnic tables. The ends of the first batch of amaretto biscotti loaves sit in a small basket on each table. Pamela pushes the basket toward Ellen, who shakes her head.

Pamela doesn't know how Ellen drinks tea without even a touch of sugar. A handful of years ago, Ellen went to Japan for her son's wedding to an Asian woman and came back with all these ideas about health foods. Pamela has never told Ellen, but she's glad her daughter hasn't married yet. She knows that Hannah is dating a man from India—or so she guesses from his dark skin. She has seen him on Hannah's porch, seen the two of them walking around Jamaica Plain, holding hands. Even though Hannah doesn't call, Pamela knows it's her duty to watch her. She hopes that Hannah moves on. Pamela doesn't think she can carry around pictures of mixed grandchildren in her purse.

The foreman Hugo walks out of his office. He pats his face with a kerchief, runs the fabric over his bald head. He never takes breaks with the rest of them. The chatter quiets. He stands at the door to the break room, shifting his weight from one foot to the other. Heather clack-clacks to a seat.

"Something's happened," Hugo says. He opens and closes his mouth several times before more words came out. "Two blasts, at the marathon. Some fuckhead put bombs in the trash cans."

People start talking at once, but Pamela can't understand them. Hugo turns on the old black stereo that sits in the cafeteria. He blows the dust from it and coughs.

A voice crackles through. "Cell phone reception has been shut down in the area. The MBTA has been suspended until further notice." The voice continues to talk, but it's lost in the waves of whispers.

The bell rings to signal the end of break. No one moves. They crowd around the radio and listen. The beating in Pamela's chest grows erratic when Hugo tells them the blast happened at the finish line, which she knows is four and a half blocks from where her daughter works as a medical receptionist. Her daughter. She needs to go to her daughter. Hannah would welcome her in all this panic.

Pamela pulls Hugo by the shoulder, away from the radio.

"I need the rest of the day off," she says. "My daughter needs me."

He leans back, as if she towers over him. "Are you crazy? It's a clusterfuck down there."

She puts a hand flat on his chest. "I need to go to her. She needs me."

He closes his mouth, swallows. He fills out a leave form, a fresh bead of sweat rolling down his bald head.

THE TEMPS ARE on Twitter and Facebook, calling out updates.

"The bombs were in trash cans."

"People have been taken to the hospital."

"Good thing the internet is still working."

"All the trains are down."

One girl sits in the corner, under her desk, her arms wrapped tightly around her knees and her eyes squeezed shut. Amit's wife—ex-wife, almost—took the same position when he'd finally confessed about Hannah.

A voice comes over the intercom: "This is a message from HR. Everyone in the Boylston Building, please make your way safely to the nearest exit. The building must be completely evacuated and will be closed until further notice." The voice repeats itself.

The temps look at Amit. He's done countless fire drills. He pictures Hannah, and the thought of her anchors him to the moment.

"This way," he says. He pulls on his trench coat. "Grab your things."

He leads them down the south side stairs and out the back entrance. Sirens and voices scramble over the brick streets.

"Stay together," he says. "You'll have to walk to South Station and catch the commuter rails home when they start running again."

They leave him as a pack, weaving through the crowd. He turns and walks the other way, toward Hannah's place in JP. When his hands shake too much, he stuffs them in his coat pockets. When his knees bend too easily, he stops and breathes solidity into them. When he hears the sirens from Boylston, he ignores them and keeps walking.

With the trains down, Amit walks the hour and a half to JP. On the stoop of Hannah's apartment in an old triple-decker house, he wonders if he should've bought something for her. Flowers or chocolates, maybe. Isn't that what he's supposed to do? What his wife had always complained about? "You're never romantic," she had said, over and over so that he can still hear her tone of voice, the hurt in it, the indignation. "You're never romantic, and sometimes I wonder if you really love me."

He hears Hannah's footsteps on the stairs before she opens the door. She's wearing the blue skirt he bought her for Christmas last year. The cerulean silk flows around her hips. He'd found it in India on a trip with his family, had doubled back to the store to buy it after dropping his wife and kids off at the in-laws' bungalow.

When Hannah hugs him, he almost chokes on the

smell of her hair. Four days have felt like months. He follows her up the steep circling stairs, trying not to look up her skirt. Even in the dim light of the single bulb, he can see the soft hairs on her legs that she has been growing out for over a year. He watches her lock the apartment door behind them and wonders what he's supposed to do now. She sits on the couch and arranges her skirt carefully over her knees. He sits at the other end. He wants her closer, wants to pluck at each of her blond curls and watch them spring back up.

"I didn't know if you'd come," she says. She keeps looking at her lap, fidgeting with a string unraveling from the silk.

He doesn't know the right response, doesn't know how to fix what has broken between them. "I wanted to see you."

She winds the string around her finger and snaps it off. "You told your wife."

"You asked me to," he says. She had pleaded, had begged him to tell his wife so that she could finally feel like a part of his life. "You wanted me to, so I did."

When he first started seeing her—two months after the pool, before they had sex—he tried to end it. He had been walking around with guilt on his shoulders, the weight of it pushing him down with each step. "I can't have my cake and eat it, too," he told her. She frowned, and said, "I'm not a cake."

Now he wonders if he should shift closer to Hannah on the couch, if she'd let him hold her hand. "I miss you," he wants to say. What he says instead is: "What a day."

Hannah clasps her hands in her lap and says nothing.

"Can I help you cook dinner?" he asks. That's what they have always done, and right now he craves a return to normalcy. He wants some way to feel close to her.

She stands up and brushes nothing off her skirt. Without a word, he follows her into the kitchen, its yellow walls making her hair even blonder, her skin even paler.

He fills a saucepan with water and turns on the

stove. They always cook the same thing. Yakisoba noodles with egg and fish sauce and a stir-fry of whatever vegetables they have on hand.

She turns off the stove. "I don't want to cook today."

He reaches out his hand and touches her waist. She steps into him. For the next fifteen minutes, he makes love to her on the floor with a desperation he hasn't felt since they were still new to each other's bodies. After he comes inside her and rolls off, she lies there and stares at the popcorn ceiling as if it were made of stars.

"What do you want?" he asks. He is sweaty and naked on the cold vinyl floor. "To do?"

"Why is it that you can't ever figure it out?"

"You wanted me to tell her, so I told her. What more do you want?"

"I shouldn't have asked you to come."

He grabs hold of one of her curls and rubs the hair between his fingers. "We can be together now. That's what we want."

"Is it?"

"I love you." He waits. He wants her to slide closer. He wants to ask her if she came, if he should fit his mouth between her thighs. "I love you," he says again. He waits. His heart races, and he is drowning. "I left my wife for you. For you."

She is silent for a long time. Then her body shivers, and he pushes up against her. She lays her head on his chest, and he strokes her hair.

PAMELA WAITS ON the stoop of Hannah's building, her finger pressing the doorbell over and over. She waited for hours at the station for the red line to start running again. She watches the hands of her watch tick by: 7:35, 7:36. On the fifth ring, she hears footsteps on the stairs. She holds a plastic grocery bag in each hand. Pamela is proud of herself. She knew exactly what to get, knows the vegetables Hannah buys every Saturday afternoon because Pamela watches her at the JP Whole Foods.

The door opens, and Hannah appears. For a

moment, Hannah's face is blank, almost pleasant, and then it twists into displeasure, and Pamela feels small.

"Mom," Hannah says. "What are you doing here?"

"I came to see you, darling." Pamela puts down one bag and hugs her daughter.

Hannah is stiff under Pamela's arms. She keeps looking back up the stairs. "I told you never to come here."

"You needed my help."

Hannah finally looks at her, searches her face.

"I brought you necessities," Pamela says. She tries to push the handle of a plastic Market Basket bag into Hannah's hand.

"I don't need your help." Hannah wraps her arms around herself and watches a group of bikers at a bar nearby.

Pamela knows her daughter is being difficult on purpose. She often did this as a child, screaming in toy stores, crying until she was allowed to stay up to watch her favorite shows. Even as a teenager,

Hannah knew the precise pitch of voice that would make Pamela see spots behind her eyes.

There are more footsteps on the stairs. The shadow of a lanky man at the door. He walks out onto the porch. Pamela recognizes him as Hannah's lover. She is surprised at the hatred that fills her.

"Everything okay?" he asks. He puts a hand on Hannah's waist, and she steps closer to him.

"This is my mother."

He is backlit by the stairwell, and Pamela can't make out his expression.

"You should go," Hannah says to Pamela.

"I'm your mother." Pamela holds out the grocery bag, but Hannah doesn't take it.

The man pulls Hannah closer. Pamela tries to ignore him, ignore the way he holds on to Hannah like he owns her, ignore his dark skin and his ink-blot eyes. The grocery-bag straps are cutting into her palms. She drops them onto the floorboards.

"Let's go upstairs," he says to Hannah. He starts to draw her back toward the foyer.

His voice grates in Pamela's ears.

"It's you," Pamela says. "You're ruining her life. You're taking her from her own mother." She tries to grab hold of his arm to pull him away from Hannah, but he flinches out of her grasp. "Get away from my daughter."

"Listen," he says. He takes a step toward Pamela. "I love your daughter."

"Amit," Hannah says. "Both of you, stop. Mom, you need to go. I told you I didn't want to see you."

Pamela bites down on her cheek to keep herself in the moment.

"Hannah, honey," she says. "Hannah. It's been long enough. Three years is long enough. I thought I lost you today. Your father and I love you."

"My father?" Breathless, Hannah's voice turns high. "How dare you."

Pamela opens her mouth to explain, but there are too many words, and they all rush toward her tongue at the same time. She ends up saying nothing. "No," she wants to say. "It's not what you think. I loved your father."

"Twenty years," Hannah says. "Did Dad know? Is that why he had a heart attack? Is that how you finally killed him?"

"Stop, Hannah."

The man rubs Hannah's back. Pamela wants to smack his hands away.

"Hannah, dear," she says. "Listen to me."

Hannah's face grows cold, shuts down like a curtain falling across a stage. "I don't care." She shivers. "You should both go."

"Baby," the man says.

"Don't you call her baby," Pamela says.

"The city's in mourning. People are dead." Hannah's voice curls louder. "What is wrong with you two?"

The man reaches for her again, but Hannah backs up into the foyer.

"Just go," Hannah says. "I want to be alone."

The man spins on his heels, walks down the porch stairs and into the night.

"Good for you," Pamela says to her daughter.

Hannah shakes her head from inside the house. She closes the door. Pamela hears the lock slide into place. Through the glass, Hannah walks up the stairs. Pamela waits until she's out of view, stacks the grocery bags up against the door, and follows the man out to the sidewalk, rubbing at the spot above her heart the way her husband used to.

ON THE NIGHT of his death, Amit Srinivasan walks down a dark street in JP. He passes a group of young bikers who laugh loudly outside a bar, propped up against their motorcycles. Amit puts his hands in his pockets and keeps walking. He tries not to think of how Hannah kicked him out. He knows her moods. He knows there is no getting to her tonight. He'll try again tomorrow.

The bikers' laughter stops. Amit looks around for cops, but the streets of JP are deserted except for young kids milling around in the pools of street-lights.

"Hey, towelhead," one of the bikers calls.

Amit keeps walking. Pamela Robertson walks a few steps behind him.

"I'm talking to you," the biker says. "They're still searching for the bomber, you know."

Amit is two blocks away from the T station. If he can get inside, he knows there will be police, at least on the train cars.

"He's trouble," Pamela says to the bikers. "He's trouble. He got my daughter in trouble."

Two men step in front of Amit. He stops. He remembers the way people looked at him after 9/11. He knows not to engage. He goes around them and keeps walking toward the station.

The man is following him, he's sure. He hears the footsteps but doesn't want to look back. Amit keeps his eyes forward. He walks faster. For the first time that night, he can see his breath coiling into the air. He hears what sounds like more than one set of footsteps behind him, but that can't be right. He chances a look. One man, tall and muscled, his hair shaved close to his head. Pamela stands behind him, watching.

Amit runs.

"Fucking terrorist cunt." The man stops, spits on the ground.

Amit keeps running and running. When he's inside the station, he finally looks back and sees Pamela tapping her card to the fare gate at the station's entrance.

Amit's breathing comes in bursts, his head full of the biker's voice and Hannah's blond hair. Something aches in his knees. He tries to think of something else. This weekend he will apologize to his wife, and she'll let him take the kids and bring them to the pond in JP. They'll rent a rowboat, and he'll row them out to see the turtles that nest on the small island. His kids will like that, especially his daughter, who once tried to make a pet out of a turtle she'd found in the backyard. He'll take them to meet Hannah.

A train rumble fills the void. Amit watches the

pigeons that fly around the station, the flapping of their wings echoing off the cement so that one bird sounds like an entire flock. The pigeons spiral up, circling around one another, up and up until the night swallows them whole.

I LIKE TO IMAGINE DAISY FROM *MRS. DALLOWAY* AS AN INDIAN WOMAN

Daisy, she thought, was a strange name. She wasn't sure she liked it. Her husband Peter had brought her to England on the promise that no one should know she was Indian. Her skin was light enough, and combined with her straight, dark hair, she could pass for an Italian, or so he thought. After all, he had to keep up appearances with his old friends, and they would be scandalized to find he'd run back home married to an Indian woman with their two dark kids.

Her name wasn't even Daisy. That was his doing as well. "A man like Peter Walsh should have a wife with a proper English name," he had told her.

It was true she had wanted to come. It was true her birth country had never been kind to her. But she missed wearing saris in the hot Calcutta summers. She missed the sound of her name in Bengali, the softness of it like warm gold, sinking one's teeth at the slightest pressure. She missed the beach, watching nervous sea-foam scuttle into the sand before the next warm wave.

She buttoned herself up in a thick wool coat. The English climate, all of this smog and chill, was starting to get to her. Peter had forbidden her to go outside. He was afraid people would catch on to the fact that she wasn't Italian if they looked at her long enough.

Now Peter had gone off to a party thrown by one of his old friends from Burton. She didn't mind his absence, but she did mind the faraway look he got whenever he talked about Mrs. Dalloway.

Outside their little house, inside a half-mile walk, she caught the tram to Piccadilly. She loved sitting inside the tram, with its smooth wooden seats and copper handrails. She felt sophisticated, wealthy. Her family back in India wouldn't even be able to imagine the kind of clean bustle she could walk through in Piccadilly Square. Motorcars with their puttering and black smoke, double-decker omnibuses in bright red, people swarming like ants from a kicked-over anthill, bicyclists trying to navigate the impossible.

If she angled her hat just right, her face fell into shadow and she could order a tea at a small shop without being recognized. She sat outside and sipped at it until it grew too cold to bear, watching all the pretty white people go about their days under the dreary London evening. What were they thinking in their pretty white heads? Ordinary people, with their ordinary suffering.

Soon it would be time for her to head back home. Her new home, with Peter in a little brick house. All the way on her walk to the tram stop, then on the tram, then all the way home, she whispered her own name to herself in Bengali, lest she forget it.

WILD ALE

My wife Adria and I are supposed to be in Europe, driving a tiny rental car from Amsterdam to the South of France, then ferrying to the Greek islands. Instead, we're self-isolating inside our third-story walk-up, a month into lockdown in response to the Covid pandemic. Adria tries to tell me it's better this way, but then again, she believes that crystals can bring luck or doom depending on the moon's cycles.

"Something terrible could've happened on our trip," she tells me. "One of us could've broken a bone. We could've been arrested. We were probably saved."

"Sure," I say, "our stuffy apartment is so much better than Mykonos."

Last month we had friends over to taste some beer I'd brewed. We smoked weed and played poker, and when the guests went home, Adria and I screamed at each other like usual before going to bed wrapped up in our drunken anger. If I'd known the country would go into quarantine shortly after, I would've tried to have a better time. Instead I fumed at our university colleague Dennis—a newly tenured professor who specializes in the literature of David Foster Wallace—who hit on Adria every chance he got. After the party, I accused Adria of inviting his flirting, and she called me a jealous tyrant.

It's a cold, bright weekend morning, and Adria is drinking her coffee and reading her daily horoscope—Gemini sun, Sagittarius rising, Virgo moon—and I'm researching the Wild Ale Challenge, a Midwest home brew competition that I've decided to enter. We sit facing each other on our green velvet chesterfield, our legs intertwined, next to the large picture window in our living room. Adria's pillowy hair catches the sun, bending light over each dark coil. She reads my horoscope—Sagittarius sun, Virgo rising, Aquarius moon—and tells me I need to watch out for bodies of water and that maybe I shouldn't take a bath tonight.

The April sun shines brilliant but somehow, there're tiny hailstones going *tink tink tink* on our windowsill. On the street below, no pedestrians, few parked cars, one biker wearing a blue medical face mask. A large pickup truck drives by with the Chicago Bears logo painted on its back window. In the truck's bed lie protest signs saying, STOP THE TYRANY! and OPEN ILLINOIS!

"What selfishness," Adria says.

"They spelled *tyranny* wrong."

We both turn back to our phones. I surf past a bunch of social media posts with the hashtag #wildalechallenge. Three weeks ago, I brewed an almond-coffee stout. Base of two-row and Munich malt, with 45 crystal, 150 crystal, roasted barley, chocolate malt, and debittered black malt. Magnum and crystal hops at 60, 30, and flameout. Wyeast

1056. Fresh brewed coffee, almond extract, and roasted blanched almonds in secondary. It'll be two weeks until I can drink it, but by all estimations, it should be good.

My next beer will be a wild ale. In the Wild Ale Challenge, you're supposed to make beer from foraged ingredients. The only thing you're allowed to buy is your grain bill. No hops. No yeast. No nutrients. No flavorings.

Down below on the street, a truck honks and someone shouts something, the words garbled by our window.

"Chili pepper IPA's ready to drink today," I say.

Adria idly scratches her eyebrow, then smooths the hairs back into place.

"IPAs are an important part of beer history," I tell her. "Did you know they were invented by the British during colonial times to survive the trip to India? The hops served as an antibacterial agent."

Adria doesn't acknowledge my factoid. On our first date during grad school, this is the kind of historical trivia I awkwardly tossed across the table as I clutched my brown ale in a smoky dive bar in Florida. Back then, Adria's eyes lit up in the dim grittiness.

The noise on the street gets louder. When we look, the Chicago Bears truck has stopped and a blonde woman is shouting down the owner of the bodega across the street.

"I want my morning croissant!" she yells.

"Online orders only." The bodega owner is calm but resolute, his arms crossed, his mask on, blocking her from going through his front door.

"This is tyranny!"

Adria sighs and rubs at her temples. "I don't know how much more I can take of this."

"I miss those croissants," I say.

Adria gives me a look like I'm a cockroach sitting on her favorite cake.

I scroll through more #wildalechallenge posts. In a few weeks, I'll ship out four bottles of my finished beer and get feedback from the judges and, maybe, win a medal. I've spent weeks tweaking my recipe, trying to nail every single weight measurement down to the hundredth decimal point.

I close my laptop. "I'm going to try the chili pepper IPA."

"It's ten in the morning, Cam." Adria takes another sip of coffee. Her mug says "hers," part of a "hers and hers" matching set we got for our wedding. The woman on the street gets in her truck and drives away.

"It's five o'clock in France," I say.

I pour a sixteen-ounce bottle for myself. A bit too much caramel flavor, but the pepper extract shines through nicely. It reminds me of our bicycle brewery tour in Denver during our honeymoon road trip across the US. We got caught in the rain and danced in the street with strangers, and every brewery had a chili pepper beer on tap. I make a note in my logbook not to add crystal 60 malt next time.

BY LUNCH, I'VE had three chili pepper IPAs and Adria's in a state. She hasn't moved from her position on our chesterfield for over an hour. She rests her chin on her hand and stares out the picture window at the empty street below. The wind whips up the accumulated hail into white snakes on the asphalt.

I sit next to her and shake her gently.

She turns to face me me like I've roused her from a deep sleep. "I wonder how many couples will get divorced during the pandemic," she says.

I imagine the millions of couples around the world, all cooped up with each other and no escape. "Why would you say that?"

"You're drunk," she says, cringing from my breath.

The bones of her shoulders jut out more sharply than they did a month ago. She's been forgetting to eat, lost in a time fog.

I'm glad the world is losing shape around me. "It's time for lunch. You need to eat," I tell her.

"What's the point?"

I go to the kitchen to heat up leftover pasta, and push the bowl into her hands.

She stares at three pieces of rigatoni speared on

her fork. "Your brewing station's taking over the kitchen. It's getting so claustrophobic in here." She stares some more at her pasta until I feed her, and even then, she only chews a couple of bites before shaking her head.

"It's just because you've been cooped up. We don't have to quarantine so strictly," I say. "We could invite over Dennis and Rhonda for some beers."

"What the fuck is wrong with you?" Adria rubs her eyes with the heels of her palms. "And you hate Dennis."

"I don't hate Dennis." Despite what she says, I know that Adria's attracted to him. I can feel it like static in the air when they're around me. But at this point, I'm willing to put up with even that for some damn company.

"He's a sweet guy," she says, and I bare my teeth. "You just want him over so you can show off your manly brewing skills and display me like a trophy and feel masculine."

"That's not true." I want her to keep talking so

that I can dissect her voice for any clues as to how she really feels about Dennis. Despite her assurances that she's done dating men, doubt clogs my throat. "You think he's sweet?"

"Stop, just stop. I can't do this."

"What do you mean by *this*?" The beer makes me reckless. Already I'm itching for another.

Adria covers her face with her hands and sobs. I think about comforting her, but my body vibrates with anger. She was the one who brought up divorces.

"You're such an asshole," she says.

I finish the pasta and have another beer. She goes back to staring at the empty street.

The fourth IPA calms me. I go to my favorite home brew site—still shipping through the pandemic—and add $3000 worth of equipment to my cart: the fully electric Bluetooth-enabled Grainfather brewing system, which can handle up to six gallons of brew, and which I can control from my phone with multi-step mashes and custom brew times; the SS Brewtech seven-gallon stainless steel conical fermenter with yeast dump valve; and a glycol temperature controller that can heat and cool up to four fermenters at a time. Three thousand dollars is more than I make per class I teach for the university. I close out of the tab without checking out and drink another beer.

Lightheaded and guilty about our fight, I wobble to Adria's crystal box and pick out two pieces of orange carnelian, which she's told me inspires and motivates. I place these crystals next to her on the couch.

I check on my mason jars. I'm trying to cultivate wild yeast for my entry in the challenge. Two weeks ago, I filled mason jars with boiled water and dry malt extract and set them outside on our balcony to collect yeast. One smells like plastic. One is growing what looks like a mushroom. I throw those out.

Adria thinks my home brew obsession is a manifestation of my inner frat boy. When we first met, she was into my butchness, but now she says I remind her too much of the "douchebag cis men" she used to date. She won't listen when I try to explain. I love brewing because at its core, it's simple: water, grain, yeast. With the world in chaos, I find calm in the pristine science of gravity readings, equipment sanitation, and hops schedules. When I brew, I can control everything. Or, nearly everything. Right now, with my ragtag DIY mash tun and my repurposed stock pot as a brew kettle, I can't keep temperatures as steady as I need to. I can't ferment at a perfect sixty-eight degrees or crash cool my beer before bottling. For that I'd need my dream $3000 system.

I make a great show of changing into my fleece-lined leggings, coat, hat, and gloves, but Adria doesn't seem to notice.

"I'll be back," I say, and put my face mask on.

Outside, I strip my coat off and stuff the hat and gloves into my pockets. I want to feel the cold sink into me. I also take off my mask, because wearing it makes me feel like something heavy is sitting on my chest.

Wind rattles the streetlights as I pass. Avoiding the

handful of others on the sidewalk, I stroll to the park down the street and pick dandelions and yarrow, which showed up after a week of good weather. I need to collect them before they die from the snowstorm predicted for tonight. I pluck whole plants—roots, leaves, and all—and stuff them into my pockets. The park is empty except for a young runner and an old Asian couple doing tai chi, all with face masks on. When they see me, the Asian couple moves away, and the runner mutters "mask-up, asshole," under her breath. I want to tell her that she's not going to catch the virus in a mostly empty park, but I still feel bad.

A truck drives by, the same one I saw earlier with the Bears logo on the back window and protest signs in the bed. The middle-aged blonde woman who yelled at the bodega owner rolls down the passenger side window and leans her head out. The truck slows to a stop in the middle of the road.

"Reopen the country!" she shouts to the four of us scattered across the park. She looks directly at me like I'm on her side. "Sacrifice the weak! The virus is a hoax!" Her face turns red from the effort.

The runner slows down to watch us. The tai chi couple turns our way. The woman waits. I wish I hadn't taken off my mask.

"Stop watching Fox News!" I shout back to her, holding a handful of plucked dandelions.

The driver of the truck is an acne-faced boy wearing all orange. He could be any one of my first-year English students at the university.

"Stay the fuck home!" I say.

The woman yells, "*You* stay home, dyke!"

The truck drives away.

THE NEXT DAY while it snows, I brew my wild-ale recipe using the dandelion greens as a hop substitute and yarrow as a way to add flavor and depth. For aroma, I add stinging nettle I found growing wild by the river where I walk every day without telling Adria. I use the same grain bill as a rye-wheat beer I brewed last summer that Adria loved: rye malt, Durst pilsner, 80 crystal, flaked rice, wheat, and rice hulls in a multirest mash. The stock pot I have isn't big enough, so I have to brew in two different pots. One boils over, the flaked rice making the wort too sticky.

Called by my screaming, Adria runs into the kitchen and finds me sitting on the floor, my head in my hands.

"Wort boiled over," I say.

Adria puts her fists on her hips. "I thought something bad had happened."

Anger rushes up inside me. I jump up and dump the whole boiled-over pot into the sink. Immediately I regret it. I've gone from five gallons to three gallons.

I lean over the sink and watch the last of the perfectly good wort spiral into the drain. I think about the Grainfather system, and how this would never have happened if I had it.

Twenty minutes and a chipotle stout later, I wash and pluck the dandelion flowers and nettle, sanitize them by dunking them in boiling water, stuff the petals and leaves into three glass carboys, and siphon the cooled wort on top. I aerate the wort and pitch yeast from the mason jars. I drink my chili pepper IPA while I brew, but I don't need the booze—brewing is the only time I don't feel like I've got glue in the veins of my heart.

By the time I'm done cleaning up, I've had a few more beers and my walk is wobbly. My anxiety about our fight yesterday, combined with losing half my brew to equipment failure, makes my stomach churn. Now that I'm not brewing anymore, it's hard to breathe right.

When I'm done, I find Adria in our shared office—her hair and makeup done, a silk button-up shirt over her sweatpants—video conferencing with her students. When the university went online and Europe was canceled, Adria agreed to teach a new critical theory class over video. She's placed carnelian, amethyst, and rose quartz on her desk outside of the camera frame. Her face has that plastic smile she wears whenever she's trying to convince someone that she's happy.

I've agreed to teach two creative writing classes for extra pay, but without face-to-face, real-time anything. I told my students it's to respect their other obligations during this time, and even dropped the buzzword *asynchronous pedagogy*, but the truth is that I can't hold any thoughts in my head except for beer recipes. I can't imagine lecturing like Adria does. I'm behind on grading, and I haven't written anything in weeks except for brewing notes in my logbook, though I'm supposed to be finishing my novel.

"When you read the assignments for next week," Adria says into the camera, "remember that Schinkel is responding not just to Benjamin but also to a large body of social science where researchers have focused on the causes of violence rather than autotelic violence."

I stand out of the video frame and watch her. We've been together for six years, but I've never gotten to watch her teach the way I have this month. She made me read that essay about autotelic violence. Violence without a direct cause or goal. Violence for the sake of violence. I remember the woman in the park, her absolute conviction and panic. My palms itch. Maybe this pandemic has made us all into assholes. At the very least, it's made us into cornered animals, hissing and spitting at the faintest shadows.

"Any final questions before we wrap up?" She notices me lurking nearby. "Oh! Look, here's Cam." She says it in a fake upbeat way that makes me cringe.

I step closer and wave to Adria's students, whose cameras are turned off in a gallery of blank gray boxes on her laptop. My usual short hair is getting shaggy around my ears, and I have dark bags under my eyes.

"It's a wild time we're living through," she says to her students, "so please remember to be kind to yourselves. Eat well. Don't leave the house. I'm here if you need me."

Adria closes her laptop and takes her earbuds out. She changes out of her nice shirt and into her usual stained tank top and worn-down sweater.

I can't help myself. "Don't leave the house?" I say. "Isn't that a bit extreme?"

"Most of my students' parents won't self-isolate," she says. "They keep going to work."

"Adria, *my* mother won't self-isolate." My mother and I aren't on the best of terms, but we still talk every week. "She said she was going to one of those protests."

Adria stares at me, her mouth open. I can feel the tirade coming. If I don't distract her, she'll try to lecture me on how to talk to my own mother.

"I finished my wild ale," I say. "Want to know what I used?"

Adria cuts me off before I can tell her about the yarrow.

"We need to pay the credit card," she says. "I just got the statement."

"Okay." My heart skips a step.

Adria puts her hands on her hips and I prepare myself.

"*Six hundred dollars* on brewing supplies?" she says. Her voice is calm and dangerous.

"I needed grain. And you know liquid yeast is better than dry. And shipping is expensive."

"You're going to brew us into poverty."

I reach for her arm but she snatches it away. I can't take her look of disdain.

"Then leave," I say. "Leave if that's what you want to do. Go fuck Dennis or something."

Adria is struck dumb. She flaps her mouth open and closed. She takes a big, rattling breath and closes her eyes. "You can't spend six hundred dollars on beer," she says. "We can't afford it."

Just to torture myself, I picture her with Dennis. I picture them laughing, Adria sitting on his lap.

"I can spend whatever the fuck I want," I say. I plop down at my desk, open my laptop, and load the home brew site where my cart still has $3000 worth of brewing equipment. "I want this stuff, I need this stuff," I say. Part of me is floating near the window, watching myself unravel. "You spend hundreds on crystals and have I complained? No." I know I should stop but I can't. The image I've conjured up of Adria and Dennis—now both naked in bed—blurs my vision. I squint at the screen, click "Check Out" and enter our credit card information. Each form element I fill in makes me breathe a little easier.

"What are you doing?" Adria screams.

From the window, I watch myself turn toward her and flip her off. I watch her incredulous face, her body tilted sideways, leaning on one hip.

Then I click "Pay Now" and it's done. In a few days, I'll get the brewing system of my dreams.

EVERY DAY, THE same Chicago Bears truck drives by midmorning. The blond woman leans out the passenger-side window to yell at whoever is on the street or in the apartments. The weather warms up enough that we have the windows open, so we hear her. Several times, Adria yells back at her, after which the woman calls us godless heathens and the truck drives away. Adria hasn't talked to me since the moment I ordered my new brewing system. I keep wondering if she'll ask me to call them and cancel the order, but she hasn't. Instead she shuts me out. She's frozen solid.

I've split my wild ale into three one-gallon containers, each with a different yeast. Every day, I sniff the air locks. I unwrap each container from its towel and look for the krausen forming on top of the wort, a sign that fermentation is healthy. But the krausen is slow to form, and when it does, it doesn't look as foamy as I expect.

"I just can't stand it," Adria says after the fifth encounter with the Bears-truck woman. Her first words to me in days, and I note that her voice is normal, as if for a moment she's forgotten. She massages her forehead with the tips of her fingers.

"People do strange things when they feel helpless," I say, quoting one of Adria's lectures.

"Thanks for the psychology lesson, Dr. Losh. Why don't you go check on your beer?"

I check on the beer. Five days after brewing, a pale film has developed on top of one of the batches. White, coin-sized bubbles form and don't pop. The air lock smells like vinegar. I move that container away from the other two. I crush a campden tablet and swirl it into the white-filmed beer, hoping to deter the infection.

"I think one of them's infected," I tell Adria.

She's lying on the couch with her laptop, scrolling through endless social media feeds.

"Hmmm," she says.

It's better than silence, so I push forward.

"Have you eaten?"

"Hmmm."

"Yes or no, have you eaten?"

"It's my stomach, my body. Stop micromanaging it. I'm not your beer."

I kneel by the couch and touch her hand. She startles as if I'd just screamed into her ear. She puts her hand on my cheek.

"I miss you," I say.

I do. I miss her like I missed salmon for the first six months after we went vegan. My body craves her. It's not just the silence in the house. Without the routine of our classes, our dinners out, our hikes, our walks by the river—she feels so far away, even when we're getting along.

"Let's just take one walk," I say. I lay my head on her stomach. "We can go down to the river."

"The horoscope said you should avoid bodies of water."

I laugh without meaning to, and she pushes my head off her.

"I'm sorry." I mean it. I'm too sober. I need a beer, or I need her touch. "I'm sorry. I want to be close to you. Please."

Adria considers me for a moment, and I think she's going to tell me to leave her alone, but instead she hugs me and pulls me onto the couch on top of her. She runs her fingers through my hair.

"Remember when you made AdriAle for my

birthday?" she says. "I loved you so much for throwing me that party."

When we were still in grad school, I brewed a raspberry sour, though I cheated on the fermentation by adding lactic acid in secondary. AdriAle and the party I threw went far toward getting Adria to fall in love with me.

We fuck on the couch. She scratches my arms so hard she leaves marks, and afterward we lie there until my fingers dry, crusted and pungent.

A FEW DAYS later, two more trucks join the Chicago Bears one, and the caravan stops for a while on our block. Six people get out and circle their parked trucks, honking and waving their signs—WE DEMAND HAIRCUTS! THE LOCKDOWN IS KILLING US, NOT COVID! DON'T RUIN MY GOLF SEASON!

Adria and I stand at our open kitchen window with our "hers and hers" coffee mugs—hers with actual coffee and mine with ground-dandelion-root tea, which is supposed to promote liver health. All down the street, neighbors stick their heads out of their windows or watch from their balconies.

"I saw a Facebook event yesterday," Adria says, fiddling with the citrine crystal she's wearing on a gold chain. We're talking again, as if things are normal. She hasn't brought up the brewing system. "They're building up to a big protest tomorrow. Calling themselves the 'unheard majority.'"

The doorbell rings, startling both of us. Since the quarantine began, we haven't had anyone ring our doorbell except for the rare package. Adria looks fearful, so I put on my mask and go downstairs to the door. It's the brewing system, delivered in three gigantic boxes at the bottom of two sets of stairs.

I drag one of the boxes up the stairs, my body rising in temperature with each step.

"What's that?" Adria asks as I haul it through the door. Her voice says she already knows what it is.

"Do you want to help me with the other boxes?"

Adria says nothing, but she comes down and helps me bring up the other two packages. The boxes take up a third of our living room. Adria stares at them from the kitchen, her hands wrapped securely around her coffee.

"Sixty thousand people are dead in the US," she says, "and you spend three thousand dollars on a fucking home brew system."

"Those things have nothing to do with each other."

Adria slams her "hers" coffee cup into the sink, where it shatters and spills its last dregs. I'm itching to open the packages, but instead I put my arms around Adria, and we stand there as the blonde woman and her friends down on the street shout, "This is China's wet dream!"

EVEN THOUGH ADRIA'S anger radiates throughout the apartment, I'm too excited to care. Instinctually, I have the urge to protect my childlike elation, to wall it away from her fury.

I open the boxes. Adria retires to the office. I run an extension cord from the living room to the closet where I put the fermenter and glycol chiller. I set up the Grainfather in the kitchen underneath our rolling butcher block island, displacing the onions, potatoes, and various pots onto the countertops.

After it's set up and sanitized, I transfer the two gallons of good wild ale into the stainless-steel fermenter for a temperature-stable second fermentation. This is when the flavors will really develop. I turn on the glycol chiller and sit there watching it run for a long time, imagining what the ale will taste like. A sweet note because of the dandelion. A bite because of the nettle. All held up by a smooth rye base. If I win this homebrew competition, I can justify spending all this on the Grainfather. If I win, I can quit teaching, take an online brewmaster course, and join a local brewery. Spending my days elbow deep in grains and yeast will keep me at peace, keep the claws of the world from wrapping themselves around my throat.

ADRIA SHAKES ME at five in the morning. I wake, half in my dream where I was putting together a recipe for a black-tea porter.

"The apartment smells like feet," she says.

I rub the sleep out of my eyes. She's right. The smell is overpowering. Saliva gathers at the back of my throat, my stomach contracting like I'm about to puke.

It takes me a few seconds before I know what's wrong. The beer. The wild ale.

I stumble out of bed and almost crash into the wall, but I catch myself. My knee rams hard into the steel bed frame. I clutch it and hobble to the closet where my fermenter is.

As soon as I open the closet door, the smell hits me, and I have to pinch my nose closed as I grope for the pull light. In the sudden brightness, I struggle with the lid of the fermenter.

When I finally get it open, the beer inside is full of unmoving white bubbles, each the size of a knuckle. The white film crawls up the sides of the fermenter, down into the beer, and all over the dandelion petals, nettle leaves, and yarrow. My knee throbs with pain. The smell is so strong I can't breathe. Something inside me breaks open like a seed, and it's not until Adria pulls me out of the closet that I realize I'm crying.

I sob into her shoulder, drenching her pajama top with tears and snot and drool. She holds me, though. When I stop crying, Adria says, "We have to get that stuff out of the house. I don't want to know how many fungal spores are floating around."

We open all the windows to the frigid night air and take the fermenter out onto the balcony.

"Shouldn't we throw this out?" Adria asks.

Even though the batch is ruined, even though it's too late to save, I can't bear the thought of dumping it.

I hug the fermentation vessel. The infected beer is still warm under my hand.

"I can't," I say, and press my face against the steel of the fermenter. Adria rolls her eyes.

Down below, the quiet, dark street sleeps before its big protest day. I imagine the blond woman with her Bears truck, her supporters at her side, all of them lost in the frenzy of their belief, shouting at the world for daring to put the health of others before their own small freedoms. All this while Adria and I burn our freedoms under our crushing sense of collective duty. I hit the side of the fermenter in frustration, and I keep hitting and hitting and hitting until that anger transforms into an idea.

"I want to put this stuff to use," I say.

Adria crouches by me and tries to pull my hands away from where they're clutching the fermenter. "What use?" She sounds exhausted.

I tell her my plan, expecting her to object, but apparently, I've worn her down. A smile creeps over her face. And just like that, it feels like we're back to before, when our love sat deep, knowledge under my doubt.

So we work, Adria and I, in the early morning as dawn breaks pink and raw on the horizon. We're out on the balcony in our winter coats, house slippers, latex gloves, and masks that shield us somewhat from the nauseating stink of toe jam. We work until the sun warms the backs of our necks and Adria has taken at least five coffee breaks. By the time the trucks arrive for their planned protest, we're ready.

This time, word's gotten out. That Facebook event that Adria saw has attracted at least twenty trucks, all parading down our street. They park in the middle of the road without hesitation. A swarm of people exits. The woman in the Chicago Bears truck has a MAGA hat and a blow horn, through which she shouts, "The revolution has begun! Socialism sucks!"

Our neighbors on the street open their windows and come out onto their balconies. The fancy RAM 1500 Limited has double speakers in its bed and starts to blast out NWA's "Fuck tha Police."

"What a weird choice of song," Adria says, drinking coffee out of the other "hers" cup.

The protesters on the street chant, "We're here, we're right! Reopen the country!"

"That doesn't even rhyme," one of our neighbors shouts from a nearby balcony.

The woman with the blow horn points it at him.

"You libtards have no idea what's happening to this country." She catches sight of Adria and me watching and wags her fingers at us. "God's brought down this wrath!"

The protesters start to chant, "We want BBQs! We want prom!"

I reach down into my five-gallon plastic fermentation bucket filled with what Adria and I spent the morning preparing: small muslin hopsacks packed with infected yeast, dandelion petals, and nettle leaves, all soaked in rank wild ale.

I chuck the first hopsack at the truck blasting music out the back. It lands with a satisfying *thunk* on the windshield, leaking greasy white film all over the glass.

Adria aims one at the blond woman with the blow horn. It misses her but lands at her feet, splashing her espadrilles and shins. There's chaos among the protesters as they try to figure out what's happening.

Above the booming music, someone shouts, "Dr. Losh?"

I freeze with another hopsack in my hand, ready to throw. Only my students call me Dr. Losh. I search the crowd, and then I see her. Maggie Carlson. My star student. She and her girlfriend are standing on one of the truck beds, pointing at me.

I lower my arm and toss the hopsack back into the bucket.

She waves at me, and I wave back. She and her girlfriend are holding a sign that says, WE WANT TO GRADUATE.

The NWA song ends, and Toby Keith's "Made in America" comes on. One of our neighbors starts playing Rage Against the Machine's "Killing in the Name" from their apartment, trying to drown out Toby Keith.

"Throw your bombs!" a neighbor shouts to us.

I stand still and try to block the view of the stink-sack-filled bucket from the street. But the neighbors don't need us to continue the attack. An older lady three doors down throws a couple of tomatoes at the trucks below, splashing a white paint job in splotches of red. Soon, many neighbors rush back into their apartments to find things to throw. Someone chucks their morning oatmeal, which plops onto a woman's head. She screams, but in the commotion, no one seems to notice. The food lands on protesters, on their trucks and signs.

Adria's hand fumbles for mine, and when I look at her, turning away from the chaos, her face is alive and wild with something I haven't seen in her in a long time.

"Autotelic violence," she says, her lips quivering into a smile.

Protesters clamor for cover, their chants forgotten, their shirts stained with rotten fruit. Many get back into their trucks and roll up their windows. My student Maggie and her girlfriend cower under a nearby awning, both splattered with eggs. Yolk glistens all over Maggie's mousy brown hair.

Adria leans back and grabs another sack of infected beer. I hesitate, but only for a moment. Buoyed by the happiness in Adria's face, I take a hop sack, and together we hurl them onto the protesters, where they splatter with stink.

I lose track of Maggie and her girlfriend, but then I spot them, running away from the commotion, pulling each other along.

We continue to throw until the trucks start their engines. The street is covered in smashed food, and I wonder, briefly, who'll clean it up. The roar of our neighbors overwhelms the din of the trucks driving away. When the Chicago Bears truck rounds the corner of the block, our neighborhood erupts in cheers.

Adria leans on the railing and laughs. She laughs and laughs. Her skin shines with sweat. I peel both our winter coats off and hug her close. I bury my face in her shoulder. We sit on the balcony with our feet dangling off the edge, listening to our neighbors go back inside their homes, the smell of rank wild ale all around us.

THE GOTH HOUSE
EXPERIMENT

By the second month of the Goth House Experiment, David wanted to shoot Oscar Wilde dead. Trouble was, Oscar Wilde was already dead. Had been since the fin de siècle. But here he was, gray and translucent in a velour smoking jacket. As David wandered through the drafty house, trying to get inspired, Wilde drifted behind him.

Wilde had appeared the very first night that David spent in the old Victorian mansion his mother left him. David had been sleeping in the biggest bedroom in the house, an oblong wood-paneled cavern with thick fleur-de-lis drapes and a curtained four-poster bed—the bed on which his mother had spent her last days, her veins clogged with cancer.

That first night after the funeral, David fell asleep in the creaking, whistling house under fresh sheets and woke to the ghostly face of Oscar Wilde hovering above him and saying, "You're in my spot."

"Excuse me?" David asked.

"That's my spot," Wilde said. "I sleep there. Though if you promise to never treat me like I'm ordinary"—and here Wilde raised a manicured eyebrow toward the other half of the bed—"you're welcome to share my bed."

If he had been more alert, David would have challenged Wilde on the assertion that ghosts sleep at all—which they don't, David found out later. But every night since then, Oscar Wilde lay down beside him on the four-poster bed. David suspected the ghost was still perfectly cogent, but Wilde wouldn't respond to most noises and would even toss about as if he were struggling to find a better position.

And so David, baffled but still monumentally

tired from moving that first day, scooted over and fell asleep on the other side while Wilde pretended to sleep in the bed with him. In the morning, Wilde was still there, even more transparent in the sunlight, smirking at David as one would at a particularly handsome onetime lover.

On David's first full day in the Goth House, Oscar Wilde followed him around from room to room, until finally David snapped. Wilde simply made a shushing motion and said, "Your mother wants me here."

"What do you mean my mother wants you here?"

"Your greatest tragedy is that you will never become her. We were friends, your mother and I."

Wilde then told David of how he'd gotten to know her in her last months, how he'd slept next to her as she faded away, how he'd promised to take care of David. David didn't know whether to believe it or not, but he didn't want to take a chance, in case Wilde was telling the truth.

From then on, Wilde stuck by David, sleeping

beside him at night, even following him to the bathroom and chattering inanely about how ghosts don't have bowel movements while David did his business. The only place in the house Wilde didn't like to go was what he called the dead poets' room—a spacious reading room in a corner of the second floor that was covered in hand-sized portraits of writers. Wilde told him the Goth House had once belonged to a baron who started a cult, and who also fancied himself a poet. This had been his death room. "He was an excellent man, the Baron," Wilde said. "He had no enemies, and his friends didn't like him. Rather tedious fellow, I always thought."

But even if David went in the dead poets' room and closed the door in order to be alone, Wilde would hover just on the other side of the door and periodically stick his head through to tell David just how selfish he was being.

On this particular late morning, two months into the Goth House Experiment, David was trying to write a poem alone in the dead poets' room. Wilde floated on the other side of the door. David could hear the ghost clearing his throat and muttering through the walls. David was hosting a salon that night, in the fashion of the goal for the Goth House—that is, to live out a decadent lifestyle in the twenty-first century, lives of the mind, drinking mead and having late-night talks about symbolism and the postmodern condition. It was what his mother would've wanted, his mother who for thirty odd years, despite being stubbornly committed to her practice as a lawyer, typed out a secret novel on a Remington 5. She had paid for David's MFA and had also made David burn her four-hundred-page manuscript in the bedroom fireplace the day before she died.

David poised his fountain pen above his open journal. Dirty New England summer light filtered through windows. He made a note on the corner of the page: *clean poet-room windows*. He sat at a large oak desk stacked with leather-bound books by Baudelaire,

Huysmans, and Rimbaud. He imagined his mother sitting right where he was, reading transcripts from depositions. The house had belonged to David's mother's third husband, which she had inherited after that husband's untimely death a few months after their wedding. When the deed passed to David, he had decided that he would move in, live here full time, and be a poet.

A drop of ink fell onto the journal page.

"Pathetic," Oscar Wilde said. Wilde had stuck his head through the wall, and the neck of a sconce was impaling his forehead like a unicorn horn.

David tried to ignore him. He had exactly five hours to write a poem for the salon.

"Not everyone has the creative faculties to be an artist," Wilde said. "Maybe you're simply a critic."

"Shut up."

David hadn't written a poem in over six months. Not a real one, anyway. He'd made an erasure poem using pages from *Brave New World* that he had hung in the entryway of the house:

London's finest
cats
glared
in silence
at
the conductor
They always
wanted
slow Malthusian Blues
but veiled
what they wanted
in ignorance

Both Alex and Julia, the only two human beings in the world David still liked, and who were the two other writers he had picked to live with him, were annoyingly prolific. If David didn't produce a good poem for tonight, everyone would know that the Goth House Experiment was a failure.

Wilde shook his head, and the neck of the sconce wobbled. "The world needs its critics."

David capped the pen and stood up. Maybe it was the house. It was too flammable. He'd gotten a letter from the city of Bedford the week after he'd moved in, with a list of renovations he would have to make for the house to pass the town's fire code. There was just too much to do, too much to fix or clean. The thick rugs had to be taken out one by one and beaten over the wrought-iron balcony railings. The stone fireplace in the dining hall needed a screen. Three crystal chandeliers had to be rewired. Every time he tried to write, he heard his mother's voice in his head, repeating to him the list of chores that had to be done now that he was master of her house.

David walked up the steep attic stairs to Alex's room. It was already past noon, but Alex often slept until evening. David needed Alex to help get the house ready for the salon.

Wilde floated behind him, fixing the gray carnation in his jacket button.

David opened Alex's door without knocking. Blackout curtains were drawn shut over the gable windows. That had been one of Alex's two conditions before agreeing to move into the Goth House: he would get blackout curtains and all of the opioid pain medication David's mother had left behind. As her cancer progressed, she had stockpiled enough fentanyl for a year, but the disease had spread through her faster than the doctors could track it, and she was dead inside of four months.

Stale smoke filled the room. Behind David, Oscar Wilde breathed in deeply.

"I do miss the singe in my lungs," Wilde said. "It's heaven to be able to buy oblivion."

David squinted through the dark. Among the clothes crumpled all over the floor, the books stacked at least seven deep on every surface, and the slab of sheepskin Alex used as a mattress, lay the rounded peaks of a white butt. Taking a couple of steps closer, David smelled the vomit that surrounded the sleeping body. Alex's breathing inflated and deflated a bubble of snot in his nose, disturbing bits of tomato in the pool of vomit.

David shook him.

Alex was completely naked, his pale body splayed out like a frog ready for dissection.

"Such a beautiful lad," Wilde said.

David shook him harder. "How can you write like this?"

"Jealousy is the pastime of the uninspired," Wilde said.

Alex groaned and blinked his eyes open.

"We need to set up for tonight," David said.

Alex blinked again.

"Such eyes," Wilde said.

"Where am I?" Alex asked.

"Home," David said. "What did you do last night?"

"No idea." Alex sat up, not bothering to cover himself. He ignored the smeared vomit all over his forearms.

"You need a poem for tonight, too. You promised everyone something new."

Alex gestured vaguely at a piece of notebook paper on the sheepskin. "Finished the last one yesterday."

"Hard work is the refuge of people who have nothing to do," Wilde said.

David picked up the paper ball and smoothed it out. Alex's handwriting—tall and spindly like he had choked out the air in between the letters—made it impossible to read more than a few words. David threw it back onto the bed.

Downstairs, Julia was waiting for David in the dead poets' room. Her mousy hair sat messily piled on top of her head, and she was wearing a dress, which meant something important had happened. In the dirty light from the Queen Anne windows, she reminded David of a picture of his mother at thirty.

"Good news," she said. "Connor said Paramount might option the first book."

Connor was Julia's agent, the one currently negotiating her two-book contract.

David tried to smile. It was painful. So he kissed her instead. Deeply. He wanted to kiss her into the wall and through the other side.

Julia pulled away. "Where's Alex?"

"He just woke up in his own vomit." David pushed a few strands of hair off her face in what he hoped was a gentle, loving gesture. "It was grotesque."

"I should check on him," she said.

"He's fine."

Wilde stuck his head in through the wall and said, "Women are meant to be loved, not understood."

She looked at the door leading toward the hall. "You should see the poem he wrote for tonight. It's hypnotic."

"You read it?" David asked.

"He showed it to me last night. While you were writing."

David attempted a smile again.

"How's your poem coming along?" she asked.

"It's done," David said. He sat at the desk, shuffling papers around, hoping that he gave off an air of casual mystery.

Julia adjusted her bun and kissed him on the forehead. He wanted to call her back as she walked away, but Wilde was shaking his disembodied head with something that looked like pity, and David thought better of it. They weren't dating, not officially. She could do whatever she wanted. He was trying not to have attachments in his life.

IT HAD BEEN Julia who had suggested the séance. David had been careful not to tell anyone about Wilde's ghost. But a week into the Goth House experiment, Julia had become fond of the dead poets' room, and she proposed a séance to call forth the spirits of long-gone poets to gather inspiration.

Alex balked at her, sitting at their breakfast nook with a plate full of waffles in the middle of the afternoon on a Tuesday.

"David just lost his mother," Alex said. "How insensitive are you?"

But Wilde nodded vigorously behind Alex's head, passing his hand back and forth through the waffle stack.

"I think it's a good idea," David said. He watched

Alex pour a splash of bourbon into each of their coffee cups. He took a large gulp. "What've we got to lose?"

They'd held it that very night, though in retrospect David admitted to himself that perhaps a séance had been a terrible idea after a full day of drinking and smoking. They pulled the drapes in the dead poets' room tight over the high-arched windows. The thinnest slice of moonlight cut a ravine through the floor. They lit a single candle and placed it near the fireplace.

Alex lay on the blue Persian rug, pressing his face into its texture. "Feels like clouds."

"Let me feel," Julia said. She got down on her belly next to him.

Wilde sighed loudly and crossed the threshold into the room. His ghostly countenance shivered as he passed through the doorframe. He took a seat by David, floating an inch above the floor.

"Are we going to do this or what?" David asked.

Alex sat up. "Of course, of course." He crossed

his legs and offered a hand to Julia and David. "I'll be the medium. I think we can all agree that I'm the most psychically open person in this group."

Alex started humming. David and Julia took his hands and hummed with him.

"Clear your minds," Alex said. "Breathe. It's all in the breathing. Breathing lifts your soul."

David ground his teeth and tried to clear his mind.

"Something is dead within all of us," Wilde said. "And what is dead is Hope."

They waited. An owl hooted outside. They hummed along with Alex, harmonizing in increments until David thought he felt the air vibrating with them. He opened his eyes. Wilde was over by the candle, trying to blow out the flame.

"Stop that," David said.

"Stop what?" Julia asked.

"Never mind. Let's keep humming."

Alex hummed. "Who are we calling first?"

"How about my good friend Mallarmé?" Wilde asked.

"Mallarmé," David said.

"We call upon the spirit of Stéphane Mallarmé," Alex said, "father of poets."

They hummed and waited. The owl kept hooting. Nothing happened. They waited and waited, calling Mallarmé's spirit and humming.

"Is your friend going to show up?" David whispered.

Wilde shrugged in a noncommittal way. "The best way to be worshipped is to die. There is no wisdom in the spirits."

After a couple of more tries, they got even drunker. At some point, Alex and Julia disappeared. David lay on the rug. He wanted to burn the house down. Instead, he called his mother's spirit and hummed. Wilde lay next to him, saying, "You're an orphan now. It's what you are. An orphan."

ON THE DAY of the salon, David worked until evening. That is, he pretended to write and stared out the window of the dead poets' room while Julia and Alex set up for the salon. David knew they would screw it up. He had given them explicit written directions, but they shooed him away every time he went to check up on them. When he asked Wilde to go and make sure all was going well, Wilde huffed and said, "I'm not your servant."

Eventually David gave up writing and went down to help. The salon would be held in the dining hall, a large space with a fresco ceiling, walls paneled in cherry wood, and three crystal chandeliers. Alex and Julia had already lit the wood-scented candles that David had bought. When he entered, Julia was kneeling on the rug by the stone fireplace, lighting a starter log that was covered in neatly cut firewood.

The dining hall had come with a long teak table, but the three of them had moved it out. Alex was now slowly dragging all of the smaller tables into the house. There was a handful already placed strategically throughout the room.

"Does this mean you're done writing?" Julia asked. She blew on the starter log.

"Yes," David said.

Wilde, floating into the room behind him, tisked.

David found the folded swatches of black silk he had bought at the fabric store. With Julia's help, he spread a piece on each table. The silk pooled over the Persian rugs and, under the candlelight, seemed to move like waves.

Over the next hour, the three of them attended to each minute element. Silver menorahs strung with crystals. Black ceramic plates small enough to fit in a palm. Neat sushi rolls catered from David's favorite restaurant (the delivery boy's eyes had gone wide and vacant at the sight of the room). Crystal goblets David's mother had bought and shipped from California. Bourbon and red wine decanted into cut glass. Tiny Bluetooth speakers hidden all around the room, playing a ghostly violin melody. By the fireplace, on a table covered in thick black velvet, a large tortoise shell painted gold. And all along one wall, floor-to-ceiling windows that opened out to an overgrown, messy garden. David had purposefully not called the landscaper his mother had recommended by way of email a few days before her death. He thought the opulence of the inside contrasted well with the chaotic nature outside. He knew it was all in the details.

By the time the first guests arrived, an hour late as David had predicted, all he had written were the three lines from that morning. Three beautiful lines—Oscar Wilde had read them over David's shoulder when they were alone and had nodded. Rather curtly, but David hadn't hoped for any more out of him. David tore the page out of his notebook, making sure to get a jagged enough edge so that people could see it in the dim candlelight. He could add to it throughout the night and read last. After all, wasn't a poem just a collection of beautiful lines? It would seem experimental and daring. Avant-garde.

He folded the page and tucked it into the inside pocket of his gray suit. He'd special ordered the suit—Italian cut, of course, with a close herringbone weave, matching vest, and trilby. Wilde watched him get dressed, nodding approvingly when he brushed himself down with a Kent brush from the 1910s.

"Those," Wilde said, pointing to a pair of black perforated wing tips.

David laced them up, put on the trilby at a slight angle, and checked himself in the mirror.

"Slick back your hair," Wilde said. "It's only unfashionable if other men do it."

David ran some pomade through his hair, noting that it was starting to thin at the top. The other day, he had counted fifteen gray hairs, though Wilde had said that the gray made him look distinguished. He put the trilby back on, smoothing the red feather tucked into the band.

"Well," Wilde said, looking him up and down, "to be popular, one must be a mediocrity."

"Why can't you ever just be supportive?"

"Now, now. Don't be cross. The guests are arriving."

Wilde followed him down the curved staircase as he made his entrance. The French doors of the dining hall were thrown open. The three of them had done a decent job, he decided, or else the candlelight hid the mistakes.

Twenty or so writers from the New England area milled around the makeshift bar table. Everyone had dropped their phones into a soundproof box in the foyer, so no one's face was lit by the glow of a screen. That, David thought, had been one of his more brilliant ideas.

"Ah, what I wouldn't give for an iced champagne," Wilde said.

Alex stood in the middle of the crowd, gesticulating wildly with a glass of whiskey. Julia leaned against the wall, talking in a low voice to Katherine, a girl from their MFA that David had been hoping they could convince into a ménage à trois. Katherine was tall and moved like a blade of grass. David walked over.

"Katherine," he said. "Thanks for coming."

Katherine smiled with her dark-stained lips. That was a good sign. She raised her glass of pinot at him and drank. Another good sign.

A crash of glass on the wood floor announced the dismissal of Alex's sobriety for the night. Julia went to help clean up, and David cursed himself for not hiring any servers. He'd wanted to hire women who would be nude living sculptures and become waitresses and maids as needed, but Julia had nixed the idea as misogynistic. He'd even offered to hire a mixture of men and women, which he thought was a fair compromise, but she had simply given him an ugly look and told him she wouldn't attend. Fiction writer or not, Julia's fancy new book deal was the reason some of their guests had agreed to come from as far away as New Haven, so David had relented.

"Are you reading tonight?" David asked.

Katherine took another sip of pinot and ran her tongue over her teeth. "How long does this go?"

Over her shoulder, Wilde was floating in the

middle of the bar table, looking moon-eyed at a young poet whose book had recently won a big prize.

"We have plenty of room if you want to stay the night," David said.

"I have work in the morning."

"Mallarmé always hosted his salons on Tuesdays."

Katherine downed her drink and gave him the glass. "Nice fedora," she said.

"It's a trilby," he said as she walked away.

A handful more guests came in, looking impressed. It was time for David's welcome speech. He made his way to the stone fireplace and cleared his throat. But the noise in the room, relentless and numbing, continued.

"You must command the room," Oscar Wilde said, floating up next to him.

"Your attention, please," David said.

"Don't beg. Command."

Alex caught his eye from across the room.

"Hey," Alex shouted.

Everyone turned to look at him.

"David has something to say."

Everyone turned to look at David. He realized he was still holding Katherine's empty goblet. "Welcome to the first mardis of the Society of Postmodern Decadent Writers," he said.

"SpoDew," Alex said.

Some people laughed. David continued.

"As neo-aesthetics, we take up the torch of our forefathers and foremothers of the fin de siècle. Our aim is to pierce through the cloud of modern drudgery toward a nobler goal. In fact, the only noble goal—Art."

Alex drunkenly pumped his fist into the air.

"Tonight we share our writings. Each artist shall attempt to stir the frozen lakes of our mundane souls. As Plato said, true Beauty should produce in us a passion so profound that it makes our very nerves sing."

Katherine chuckled into her hand and whispered something to Julia. The two women bent their heads together.

"Actually," Wilde said, "both Plato and Plotinus viewed passion as an essential component of Beauty. In fact, my dear colleague Walter Pater perhaps said it best . . ."

"Fuck off," David said.

The guests looked at each other, confused. Someone laughed.

"This—this is a place to talk about literature," David said. The words were starting to leak out of his head. "And . . . and . . . and about our own writings."

The guests stared at him. Katherine was still whispering something to Julia, whose face was full of pity.

"Shots!" Alex said.

The guests turned back toward the bar. Conversation started again like a faltering engine.

"That was only slightly painful," Wilde said. "I'm sure everyone will remember."

David fished a pipe out of the pocket of Alex's coat hanging haphazardly on a high-backed chair. Alex believed smoking fentanyl was the safest way to get high. David took a hit.

"Opium?" Wilde asked. "Best cure."

David chewed on the pipe. He'd been meaning to look up exorcisms again but hadn't gotten around to it.

"Do you actually know my mother?" David asked. He took another hit. The beating in his chest didn't calm. "Be honest."

"Writers!" Alex shouted from atop a small, spindly table that rocked back and forth with his weight. He had another whiskey glass in one hand and a piece of crumpled paper in the other.

The guests quieted.

Alex balanced on the table and read, his breathing heavy, his hands shaking, his words a little slurred. But it was beautiful. His lines landed, and David watched the guests gasp and laugh at all the right moments. Even Wilde stopped ogling the prize-winning poet and stood so still that the tips of his feet brushed the ground.

When Alex finished, the guests all clapped. David turned back toward the fireplace and took another hit. He felt every corner of the folded-up paper in his pocket beating along with his heart that wouldn't slow down. The flames tilted and blurred. The readings continued. Julia, Katherine, the prize-winning poet, so many others who had won awards and for whom writing just came easy. David hated them all. Under their words, his three lines were nothing. *He* was nothing. He took more hits, and the walls melted away.

"You should be careful with that," Wilde said.

"No one asked you," David said.

"Your mother wants you to be careful."

David watched the flames make a conga line this way and that, and for a moment, the redness stitched together into a wavering image of his mother's face, not wasted—cadaverous and sunken—like it had been when she died but full and nodding, saying something to him. She was holding her mouth like she'd tasted something sour. He crouched down on the rug near the fireplace.

"What do you see?" Wilde asked.

His mother's face sputtered, flickered, disappeared. David threw the pipe into the fireplace, where it landed with a *thunk* and a *hiss*.

"Now, now," Wilde said. "You'll never be an artist with that temperament."

Julia walked up, asked him if he was okay. In response, David pulled her into the darkest corner and kissed her so hard that the straps of her dress fell away. The fentanyl had numbed him. He could barely feel her lips. Her face was close and yelling something, but he couldn't focus on the words, just the volume of her voice circling him, squeezing into his pores.

Someone pulled Julia away from him. Alex.

David pushed Alex hard, sending him stumbling backward past the fireplace. In a series of quick flailing kicks, Alex scattered the pile of burning wood onto the rug.

Wilde tried to catch him, but Alex fell through and landed on the floor. David thought he saw his mother again behind the commotion, in the fire. The flames expanded outside the bounds of their stone enclosure, engulfing the rug on the floor. Her lips moved as if she was trying to talk. But the room was too chaotic, too loud for him to hear.

"Get out," David shouted. "Everyone. Get the fuck out of my house."

The guests were running, clamoring everywhere, coughing from the smoke. People everywhere scattered to the wind like so much pollen. The rug fire spread to a table, where it flashed onto the silk cloth.

"Get out, I said!"

The guests ran out through the doors, their screams buzzing in a fog close to the floor. The gold tortoise shell shivered in the fire. His mother was still in the flames, still talking.

"David, come on." Julia's voice, and her face materialized next to him. "Time to go."

He almost got up, but Alex appeared on her other side. "Let's go, buddy."

"Get out, both of you," David said. "I'm giving you what you want."

"You're just high, David." Julia reached out for him, but he smacked her hand away.

Alex took Julia's elbow.

"Go," David said. The anger that had catapulted him was gone, dissipating into the night. His mother's face was fading. "Please," he said, "just go."

Still holding her elbow, Alex steered Julia out the door.

David sat in front of the burning table. His mother was gone, lost to the flames. Somewhere far away, sirens. He took the notebook paper out of his pocket with his three lines. Wilde sat down next to him.

"A truly decadent party if I ever saw one," Wilde said. "I'm almost jealous."

"You don't know my mother," David said. "You lied to me."

Wilde shook his head but didn't answer. The tortoise shell was burning, its gold paint fuming in a column of smoke.

David read his three lines out loud into the empty room:

I spin around you like a glass moon you breathed into life
We lack synchronicity, orbits beating out of time
Tell me who doesn't believe in infinity

Only cicada music and scorching wood answered. Wilde stayed quiet. David crumpled up the paper and threw it into the flames, and they both watched the words burn into dust.

MIRACLE BOY

I sat behind him the day he grew wings. I always seemed to be behind him—in class, in line during morning prayer—maybe that's why I noticed him in the first place, before the wings, before everyone else did.

He was in my third-grade class. Red sand always coated his legs, garish against his tea-colored skin. He took off his shoes to play in the courtyard at recess and kicked up the sand where grass refused to grow under the tropical Sri Lankan sun. His friends played cricket. They ran and yelled and boasted under the watchful eyes of the girls who stood by the swings. But he just kicked and kicked at the sand, watching the dusty clouds his feet made.

My body wasn't strong enough to play outside at recess, so I sat at the classroom window and watched his feet, the way the sand slowly stained their bright, pink undersides.

His name wasn't Peter. That's just what everyone called him after his wings grew in. Peter, because the white downy wings made him look like an angel. Peter, because after he grew wings, his mother converted and joined the Pentecostal church in front of our school. Peter, because everyone forgot what his name used to be.

I know now that in the Bible, Peter isn't an angel. We should've called him Gabriel. But Peter was the most popular Christian name in a town full of Hindus who had never even seen a Bible, so Peter was the name that stuck.

Every morning before the wings, he stood three rows up from me during prayer, when we would gather with all the other Hindu kids. The Christian students went to mass in the church across the street, and the Muslim students prayed in the empty gymnasium where they could lay out their prayer rugs.

That early in the morning, I felt strong enough to stand in line. I drank the raw egg that my mother had cracked into my coffee before breakfast in the hope that the protein would fill up my shrinking body. I stood at morning prayer with my heart jumping in a rhythmless pace and watched Peter eyeing the sand. He shifted his weight and held his fists at his sides, holding in the urge to kick it away into a dust cloud that floated up and up and up.

THE DAY THAT Peter grew wings, I sat behind him in class, watching the way his shoulder blades pushed at the white fabric of his uniform shirt. A little pool of sweat formed along his spine.

Miss Virginia wrote long division, her chalk clicking against the board, the tail of her white sari trembling with each movement. She barked out our names one by one. For right answers, she gave a tight nod of her head as she whipped around to scratch chalk on the board. For every wrong answer, the student had to walk up to her and present a hand, palm turned upward. She rapped it three times with her wooden ruler.

She called on me. I kept my eyes on the sweat creeping up Peter's back and fought off the way the classroom blurred. I gave the answer I had scribbled on my graph paper. Miss Virginia nodded and went back to the board.

She called his name. His shoulder blades rippled as he sat up straighter. His voice quavered. Wrong answer.

He walked slowly up to her as she tapped her Bata slippers against the cement floor. He held out his left hand, palm facing upward. Sand coated his legs up to his knees.

Miss Virginia brought her ruler down on his hand. He flinched with his whole body and whimpered at the back of his throat. The force of it knocked him backward, twisting his shoulders and back as if he were about to fold in two.

The ruler came down again with a sharp *crack*. His back popped open like a ball of yarn come undone. His crisp white shirt ripped. His shoulder blades shot out, white and slimy with blood.

Miss Virginia stumbled back and covered her mouth with her hand. One of the girls in the class screamed. I clutched the edge of my desk. The walls tilted, and I hoped I was still sitting upright. A sharp pain poked me in the chest. No one else moved. Miss Virginia brought the ruler down again. *Crack*.

His little body convulsed. His bones grew and bent downward.

Crack, *crack*, went the ruler. Fuzzy little feathers sprouted on the bones and filled in. *Crack*, and he had wings. White feathers coated the floor near him. Miss Virginia stood in front of him with the ruler. Her mouth hung open, and her body heaved. She fell to her knees, her sari pooling around her.

AFTER THAT DAY, I didn't see him for two weeks. My skin turned cold, and I wasn't strong enough to go to school. At night I closed my eyes and watched him leave again and again through the school court-yard, the red sand puffing up around his feet with each step, his wings gleaming in the hot sun. Even his mother was too afraid to walk near him. He walked in a space all his own, his back stiff, his starched white shirt hanging in two strips from his shoulders.

When I showed up to school again, Peter had a new name and golden hair, the kind of hair we saw only on white Red Cross workers and actors on TV. He didn't come to morning prayer but showed up afterward in class, trailing behind the Christian stu-dents. The other kids avoided him. Miss Virginia wouldn't look at him and never called on him in class. We all took our turns with the ruler, but he was allowed to sit on a stool in the back, writing quietly. The other kids had already started calling him Peter.

At recess he stood in the shade of a mango tree and watched the other boys play cricket. He curled his toes into the sand, then straightened them again.

When one of the boys hit a sixer, the ball ricocheted off a branch of the mango tree and fell at Peter's feet. He leaned down and picked it up, his wings unfurling to match the shift in weight.

The boys stopped playing. They stared at Peter and his new blond hair. One of the Christian boys drew himself up and walked down the field to the mango tree. He held out a bony arm, and Peter dropped the ball into it. The boy bowed his head. Peter's wings shook themselves. A few feathers floated to the ground and into the sand.

A few days later, the three Christian boys in our class clustered around Peter. They followed him back from morning mass at the church across the street from the school, and again from the school to evening mass. They sat around his stool at the back of the class. When he stood under the shade of the mango tree, they sat at his feet.

Miss Virginia didn't call any of them to answer questions. They didn't talk. Silence trailed behind them.

Parents began to linger after dropping their kids off in the mornings, loitering outside the wrought iron gates of the campus to catch a glimpse of Peter.

One day, a bully in our class taunted Peter. Krishna the bully, large faced and gangly armed, was a year older than the rest of the kids in our grade because he had been held back. He pointed at Peter under the mango tree at recess.

"You're a demon child," Krishna said.

The other kids stopped playing. Krishna had broken the silence that Peter and his wings demanded.

"You're a demon child," Krishna said again. He put his hands on his thin hips and looked around at the crowd of kids.

I watched through the classroom window, nursing a light dizziness and hoping that Krishna wouldn't see me, one of his usual targets. My body offered a variety of opportunities for him to poke fun: my pale skin that he said made me look yellow; the way my muscles sometimes refused to work like they should, giving me a limp when I walked or ran; the fact that I often had to stay inside during recess because I wasn't strong enough to even breathe normally.

I rubbed at the spot where my chest hurt.

Peter didn't turn around. He continued to watch the cricket game, though the boys had stopped playing and had turned their attention to Krishna.

The three Christian boys flanked Peter and stared Krishna down. Krishna walked toward them, his hands never leaving the sides of his uniform shorts.

Anton, small and soft with a nose like a crow's beak, balled up his fist and shook it. Peter didn't turn around, but his wings shivered and shook loose some white feathers that floated to the ground.

Krishna stopped a few yards away from the mango tree and pointed a thick finger at Peter.

"Demon child!"

Anton ran at Krishna, his small fist flying, his face pulled in tight toward his nose. Krishna's hands dropped from his hips and rose up to catch Anton's fist. With one hit from Krishna, little Anton fell, his body sending up a cloud of red.

Peter's wings unfolded above his head, whipping him around, shaking the branches of the mango tree. The wings stretched out behind him, gathering the air, and snapped forward, sending wind gushing toward Krishna. The wings flapped once, twice, three times. Air and sand lashed around Peter.

Krishna stepped back. He shielded his eyes against the wind and ran.

Peter's wings stopped flapping and folded back behind his body. Anton lay still on the ground, his head nestled in between rocks. A white feather landed on his chest.

Anton coughed.

Peter's two other boys knelt down, scooped up more and more of the feathers that had fallen, and dumped them on the fallen boy. Feathers and sand, and little Anton coughed and coughed and sat up.

This was Peter's first miracle.

THE NEXT DAY at school, I heard a rumor from my best friend Meena, who had heard it from another girl in our class, who had heard it from her mother, that Peter had given one of his feathers to the home-less man who stood outside of the Hindu temple near our school. We knew of this man, with his crutches and the dirty bandages wrapped around his legs. But after Peter had given him one of his feathers, the man disappeared from his usual haunt, and the rumor went that his leg had been cured, that he had cleaned up, converted, and now had a job cleaning the pews at Peter's church.

I wasn't convinced. Anton could've sat up anyway. There was no saying that the feathers were involved. And the man from the temple—well, no one had seen him at the church without his bandages and crutches, and until someone did, this was just a rumor.

But everyone else seemed to go along with it. More and more parents, and even some of the local towns-people, hung about the school gates. The school's new security guard eyed them all day, his hand on the baton that he was allowed to carry. A tea shop down the street sent its delivery boy running back and forth to the gates of the school, carrying sweet tea in little glass cups for the crowd.

The crowd parted for Peter and the three Christian boys when they went to the church across the street, no one daring to come too close to the wings. The Hindu and Muslim women hung back even farther, on the edges of the throng, whispering behind hands and the frayed tails of their saris.

ONE DAY PETER and the other Christian boys didn't show up to class after morning mass. We watched through the classroom windows that faced the courtyard while Miss Virginia went to fetch them.

Peter stood on the church steps with his wings folded behind him, flanked by his mother and a priest in a white robe, facing the crowd that had gathered between the church and the school. The boys stood off to the side. The dark mouth of the church looked, for a moment, like it would swallow them.

A man broke free of the crowd and carried a little

girl up the church steps. He laid her down by Peter's feet.

Peter's mother stroked one of his wings. It unfolded and stretched out. With one yank, she plucked out a feather. The wing folded itself back up. She handed the feather to the man, who placed it on the little girl's chest.

We waited.

"She moved," one of my classmates said.

I tried to squint to see, but the little girl at Peter's feet was too far away to notice movement.

"She moved."

I still couldn't see anything, but my classmates pointed excitedly at the little girl who hadn't moved.

The man in front of Peter fell at his feet, and the crowd cheered.

THE MONSOON CLOUDS chased each other out of town. The sun drummed on our heads when we stood in morning prayer. Peter's place in line was empty, as if his wingless body had left imprints in the sand. No breeze came from the ocean. The sand got dustier and settled into the space between our toes.

Peter stopped standing by the mango tree at recess. Instead, he went out the school gates, stood on the church steps with his mother, and entertained petitioners. The tea shop made a roaring trade.

Every day Peter performed a new miracle. His mother plucked a feather off a wing and bestowed it on each petitioner. Often the petitioners brought gifts—clothes, sweets, sometimes small pieces of jewelry. They laid these at Peter's feet, and Peter's three Christian boys gathered them up under the watchful eye of Peter's mother and the white-robed priest.

Many days passed before anyone noticed that Peter's feathers weren't growing back. The stark white skin over the bones of his wings started to show where Peter's mother had plucked too many feathers. She became more and more selective. Meena's aunt, who had seizures, was turned away. Miss Virginia's nephew got a feather, but only because he had been in a coma for a month. The size of petitioners' gifts doubled, then tripled in the space of a week. Some people tried to buy Peter's feathers. Sometimes it worked. There was a rumor that Mrs. Chandra, the Hindu widower of the once-richest man in town, got a feather for her Muslim housekeeper's son, who was almost five years old but hadn't said a word.

I listened to my parents at night when they thought I was asleep. They wanted a healthy kid, but no matter how much they prayed to the gods and goddesses at the temple, and no matter how many doctors we waited in line for at the free hospitals, I didn't get better. My body continued to shrink. My heart beat erratically, sometimes painfully. My mother wanted my father to petition Peter.

"We don't have anything to give," my father said. "They'd turn us away. We'd be humiliated."

I wanted to tell them it wouldn't work. I wanted to tell them it was all lies, that Anton would've gotten up anyway and that the paralyzed little girl hadn't actually moved. Instead, I shivered underneath my heavy blankets. My nails had started turning yellow, and my lungs wouldn't fill even when I drank down the air. And I thought maybe, just maybe a feather couldn't hurt.

AFTER THAT, I watched the front of the church closely, wondering if I would see my father's graceful body climbing up the church steps to kneel at Peter's feet.

When I'd imagined the scene in my head, I hadn't imagined rain. I hadn't imagined a crowd soaked through to the bone, taking shelter under newspapers and the overhang of school buildings, people pressed up against the walls of the school, black umbrellas held against the onslaught of the second monsoon season. My classmates stayed inside for recess, watching Peter on the church steps.

My father's yellow shirt clung to his back, his muscles visible underneath the wet fabric. Even from the classroom, I recognized the way his shoulders rolled forward and back as he climbed the steps.

Peter and his mother stood at the open mouth of the church doors, dry under the awning. My father squared his shoulders. Slowly, stiffly he fell to his knees. He spread out his hands and looked up at Peter. He was too far away to hear over the steady drum of rain.

Peter's wings unfolded and extended themselves. The feathers hung ragged and limp. The tip of a wing tapped Peter's mother in the arm, but she didn't pluck out a feather.

The priest walked out through the church doors, his white robe wet at the hem.

The wings snapped shut.

The priest puffed out his stomach and said, loud enough that we could hear him at the school, "Only members of this church, followers of the Lord, can receive the blessings of our angel."

My father's hands dropped to his knees. The crowd swelled with silence. He looked up at Peter. The wings trembled but stayed folded.

Thunder boomed. The lightning got brighter, and the crowd swayed on its feet.

My father put his hands up, still on his knees, praying to Peter. Even under the gray clouds, Peter's new golden hair shimmered. The wings opened again, unfolding behind Peter's little body as if he were going to take flight.

Peter's mother turned to the priest, who raised his hands as if he were going to gather up the crowd in his embrace. The three Christian boys shrunk back into the dark mouth of the church.

"Only members of the church," the priest said again in his booming voice, "can receive the blessings of our angel."

My father pushed himself off the ground and stood, solid.

The crowd pushed closer to the church steps, umbrellas held tight. The wind howled through the spaces between bodies.

Peter's wings hung, statue-like, in the air.

Someone shouted from the mob. Other voices joined in, their words lost to the wind.

"I'm going to go see," Miss Virginia said. "Everyone stay here."

She took her umbrella and walked out into the

rain. She weaved through the densely packed crowd but didn't make it to the stone church steps. The crowd closer to Peter was too dense to let her through.

"Let's go see, too," one of my classmates said.

"She said to stay," said another.

"Well, I'm going."

For a tense moment, no one moved. Then a couple of kids walked toward the door. I stood at the window. I didn't want to face my father in the rain. I didn't want to hear him plead with Peter. But I didn't want to be left alone, either, and my classmates moved as a whole. If one went, we were all going. I joined them at the door.

The cold rain bounced off us and into our uniforms. We shivered and moved as one unit, in a long trail like a snake, toward the front gates. The lightning distracted the guard, and we wound our way through. My legs refused to move at a normal pace. I held up the line, and we scattered. We squeezed our small selves in between the others, but the crowd ground us to a stop.

Voices grew more distinct. Snippets of sentences floated to me.

"He belongs to all of us," someone said.

"All of us," others echoed.

The priest took a step toward the crowd but stayed dry under the awning.

"He belongs to this church!" the priest said.

I stood in the thick of the mob—people crushed me from all sides, blocking out most of the rain. The wet sand ate my slippers.

"All of us deserve feathers."

My father stood in front of Peter and looked down at the quivering wings.

"Members of this church—"

"All of us."

My head spun, and my heart jumped to the thunder. I swayed with the crowd.

My father reached out his hand and stroked the top of one wing, slowly, following the direction of the feathers down to the very tip.

I tried to push at the crowd to get to my father, but

the bodies around me wouldn't budge. I wanted to shout, but my voice clenched around the pain in my chest and did not leave my body. I struggled to keep my head up.

My father looked out over the crowd. His eyes swept over me. As if pulled, I stumbled forward, through a break in the throng.

I made my way up the steps as everyone watched. Peter looked at me, his wings shivering with anticipation. Before anyone could stop me, I moved close, grabbed a feather from the wing, and yanked it out.

The crowd's cheer answered the rumble in the clouds.

The priest tried to snatch the feather away. My father was faster, picking me up, stepping back into the rain and down the steps. The crowd swallowed him, cheering still. It surged against the stone steps until the very edge of it moved to the open mouth of the church and engulfed Peter.

Peter's wings lifted up and beat air and rain at everyone around him.

My father put me on his shoulders and bore through the horde, away from the church and the school. I strained to keep sight of Peter, his feather gripped in my fingers.

As a mass, the crowd pulled Peter into the rain. Thunder clapped, and the wings beat at the sky. The arms of the crowd reined in the wings and pulled Peter to the ground. Peter's mother and Miss Virginia tried feebly to push their way to him. The priest stood in the open mouth of the church and watched.

I struggled against my father's hold, but my head was too dizzy, too full of thunder.

"You're going to be healed," my father said. He held me tighter and pushed through the crowd.

Umbrellas tumbled away, abandoned. Peter kicked at the sand, but the rain had already drummed it into the ground. I clutched the feather, the shaft's oil and blood seeping onto my fingers. Behind me, lightning split faces into shadows. The crowd swayed to the thunder as it plucked and plucked and plucked at the wings.

PREVIOUSLY PUBLISHED

"Patriots' Day" appeared in *Fifth Wednesday Journal*.

"I Like to Imagine Daisy from *Mrs. Dalloway* as an Indian Woman" appeared in *apt*.

"Wild Ale" appeared in Electric Literatur*e*.

"The Goth House Experiment" appeared in Queen Mob's Teahouse.

"Miracle Boy" appeared in *Fiction Vortex*.

LAND ACKNOWLEDGMENT

At this book's publication, I reside on traditional Powhatan lands, in the Monacan Nation in Tsenacomoco, which is now known as Virginia. I seek to honor the history of this land and to recognize and acknowledge the Indigenous people who are still here and who are trying to improve the world for future generations. Please read and support Indigenous authors, such as Kateri Akiwenzie-Damm, Kenzie Allen, Cherie Dimaline, Louise Erdrich, Brandon Hobson, Randy Lundy, Tommy Orange, and Tommy Pico, among others. I also urge all of us to learn more about the histories and contemporary realities of the traditional Indigenous stewards of the lands in which we live and work. We need to ensure that land acknowledgments such as this one are not just empty gestures but are supported by meaningful actions toward justice and peace for Indigenous peoples and toward forging healthy relationships between the land and the peoples who call it home.

Thank you to Kateri Akiwenzie-Damm and Randy Lundy for their advice and guidance in writing this land acknowledgment.

ACKNOWLEDGMENTS

This book has been a long time in the making, and I'm indebted to the support of so many people, including the mentors in whose workshops many of these stories were written: Tony Amato, Mark Winegardner, Elizabeth Stuckey-French, Jennine Capó Crucet, and Skip Horack. And thank you also to my instructors and professors at the University of Nebraska-Lincoln, who taught me how to write in the first place: Amelia Montes, Timothy Schaffert, Joy Casto, Judy Slater, Daryl Farmer, and Jonis Agee.

Thank you to the many people who have read and responded to these stories over the last decade, but especially to Billy Hallal, Noah Farberman, Patrick Cottrell, Daniel Tysdal, Namratta Poddar, and my writing group SLCK—Laurel Lathrop, Colleen Mayo, and Karen Tucker—without whose support and careful feedback this book would be in much poorer shape.

Thank you to Diane Goettel, who first suggested to me the idea that this could be a book.

Thank you to my agent, Erin Harris, and to my editor, Mark Doten, and to the whole team at Soho Press for believing in me. And also to Sonali Chanchani for helping me place some of these stories.

Thank you to my family for standing by me, especially Amma, Appa, Varun, Courtenay, Linda, and Jeff (who also provided editorial feedback). Thank you to my friends who have supported me wholeheartedly. You are the foundation that allows me to explore and take risks.

Thank you especially to Sam, my rock. You deserve only endless joy.

Thank you to my partner in life and all things, Geoff Bouvier, for everything.

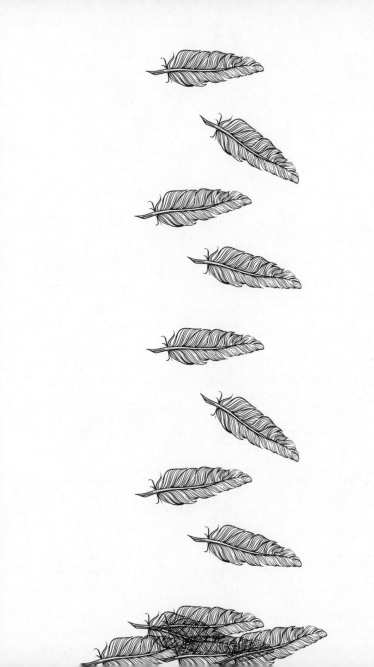